THE LEGEND OF THE SHIP CAPTAIN'S BOX

Gary Griffith

Garitage Books
SONOMA, CA

Garitage Books
P.O.Box 436
Vineburg, CA 95487

Publisher's Note: This is a work of fiction. Names, characters, places, and incidents are a product of the author's imagination. Locales and public names are sometimes used for atmospheric purposes. Any resemblance to actual people, living or dead, or to businesses, companies, events, institutions, or locales is completely coincidental.

Book Layout ©2015 The Book Makers.
Editor: Teja Watson—Two Birds Editing
Cover photo used by permission www.hygra.com Antique Boxes.

Ordering Information:
Quantity sales. Special discounts are available on quantity purchases by corporations, associations, and others. For details, contact the "Special Sales Department" at the address above.

The Legend of the Ship Captain's Box/ Gary Griffith. -- 1st ed.

Ingram Spark Print ISBN: 978-0-9961961-0-9

Apple iBooks eBook ISBN: 978-0-9961961-1-6

Create Space Print ISBN: 978-0-9961961-2-3

Kindle eBook ISBN: 978-0-9961961-3-0

For my parents, Bill and Arline

and my children

Jeramy, Kayleigh and Maggie

1

—George Elliot

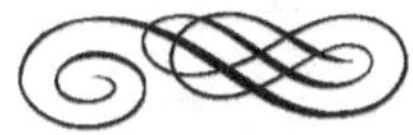

The past began whispering and it slowly wrapped itself around a lone fencepost in a pasture of regret.

Leah sat her tea on the table and saw the headlines in Frances's lap. The print bold and pronounced, bounced off the page at her as she read: FIVE FAMILY MEMBERS PERISH IN HORRIFIC CRASH.

"Can I bring you anything else Frances, a blanket perhaps?"

When the silence crept back onto the veranda, she said, without raising her head, "What did you say Leah?"

"I brought you your tea. Would you care for anything else, perhaps a blanket?" Leah now noticed several tears blotting onto the old newspaper, stained with age. The photo showed a crowd gathered at the top of a deep gully and the caption read; *the car, an accordion pleated mass of twisted metal lay where eight-year-old Billy Hendrix found the mangled wreckage Saturday.*

Frances began to cough her raspy, dry hack and Leah handed her a tissue.

"A blanket? No thank you, I am enjoying it out here this morning. It must be ready for spring to arrive because I can feel it in my bones. My granddaughter and her children are coming soon. She hasn't been around in a while."

"It will be nice for you to see them. I'm going inside to attack those breakfast dishes. Just push that button on your wrist if you need me."

She settled her frail body back into her wheelchair staring at the headlines and said to herself, *I am sorry I pushed you away, Vanessa, I was so consumed in my own grief, I lost you somehow. I burnt the dinner, didn't I? I missed my twins, their spouses and Emily. I wallowed in my own depression for so long, bathed in it, when you needed me so much. I have been such an ornery mule.* Raising her head from the clipping, she took in a long gaze down slope to the linear row of Canary Island Palms to the river and her mind meandered into the past, *her granddaughters racing their horses out of the barn, down the lane to the river to swim in the summer. They both hated their piano lessons but eventually became gifted at it.*

She interrupted the silence and said aloud, "I never told them how proud I was of them." Her head swayed in dismay and said, "Frances, you allowed yourself to be a grumpy old woman and it became a habit."

An Anna's hummingbird began to scout the trumpet vine on the veranda, which was reaching east. Her thoughts, now bathing in the bird's musical hum, its scarlet coat and wings of harlequin dancing in the morning sun and said to the bird, "Good morning Claire, yes I know, I must make it right, it is time."

She folded the faded news clipping, placing it in her folder and placed her tablet on her lap and with her shaking arthritic hand, took her thoughts into the morning breeze and began to write.

March 11, 1997
My Dearest Vanessa,

If you are reading this letter, I am in another place. No worries, I am fine. I want you to know that I love you, Vanessa, and your chickabiddies, so terribly much. I am writing this to you because I know my fate awaits me with every one of my breaths, I feel it deep inside waiting.

There is a ship captain's box in a hidden passageway in my home and it holds the story of my great-Grammy Claire. This box traveled to California with her at the beginning of the gold rush and holds her story about traveling in a steamship around Cape Horn to California and the many challenges she faced once arriving in San Francisco. In case something happened to me before your visit, I didn't want to leave you and your children without her story. Like Maeve, I wanted to interview my Great-Grammy Claire. At the time, she was near the end of her life and had not finished her story. She promised me she would finish her story someday. Unfortunately, she died before finishing it. I learned that she and my great-grandfather were true adventurers and they had a passion for adventure, discovery, love, and family.

The last challenge of the box took me years to discover. There are six secret compartments in the box, where you will find my Great-Grammy Claire's story of the man she loved and lost, along with her most prized possessions. I had hoped for years to add the last pages she wrote to her book, but then I could not physically get to the box. Sometimes life just gets in the way and sometimes life just walks out the door.

Vanessa, I am so very sorry about the way I have acted toward you after your parents died. All that was good in my heart, I guess, just dried up. I am embarrassed by my behavior and I hope that you could find it in your heart to somehow forgive me.

My longtime friend David Birkshire will be contacting you, as he is the executor of my estate. Watuppa Grove is now under your loving care. Following your dreams is important Vanessa, and I know you will teach that to your children, so they too can find their voice and their sacred place in the world.

I love you Vanessa and your chickabiddies,
Grammy

2

Scars have the strange power to remind us that our past is real.

—CORMAC MCCARTHY

March 9, 1997

Vanessa found her thoughts wedged between despair and redemption. She knew what needed to be done yet her past kept confronting her future.

Grammy Frances used to call her chickabiddy. She does not call her chickabiddy any longer. When Vanessa was fifteen years old, she stopped. In fact, Grammy pretty much stopped everything by the time the crash came along. Vanessa remembered her Grammy wailing between her own heaving sobs. Everything important in their lives vanished. Vanessa lost her parents, aunt, uncle and her cousin Emily and her Grammy lost her children and her granddaughter in that one horrible moment.

After the funeral, the reception was at the family home, Watuppa Grove. As Vanessa sat in the porch swing, she gazed out to the river, into the fading light in the amber of winter. She wrestled with her childhood memories: playing in the barn on the rope swing, with her cousin Emily, for hours, while the odor of manure and feed hovered over their senses and butterflies tickled their stomachs; waking up on Christmas morning with hot chocolate and sticky buns;

riding horses in the woods. Now everything morphed into her own silent shadows.

Grammy, her skin bunched around her red, swollen eyes, carried a pained stare throughout the reception. The one thing she said to her granddaughter was, "Your father loved Watuppa Grove and I see that in you, and now you are all I have left of your father." It was if Grammy was trying to peel off her father's layer of the onion, and discovered Vanessa there. At that moment, Vanessa felt naked without her parents.

Vanessa and her Grammy were all that now remained of the family. And Grammy slowly drifted away from her granddaughter, becoming over time a cantankerous and insensitive old woman. Because of this, Vanessa's heart camped on the perimeter of anger and something lost. Over time, the empty space that separated Vanessa from her Grammy grew into a deep canyon.

First came Maeve and then Brodie, her two little lovelies, she called them. The birth of her children began to fill the painful abyss in her life, and in time Vanessa began to carve a new path with her children.

It took Vanessa three days to collect her courage to call her Grammy to ask if Maeve could interview her for her California Gold Rush project. She spent those days running random scenarios in her mind, most of which leaned south of positive. How would Maeve and Brodie react if Grammy became insensitive to them? How would Vanessa herself react? Finally, with measured courage, Vanessa made the call.

"Hi, Grammy! This is Vanessa."

"Yes, I know who you are."

"The kids and I have missed you. How are things? Your health?"

"I am 98 years old and I am tired, so is my health."

"Well, Maeve is hoping she might interview our family gold rush expert for her fourth grade California Gold Rush project."

"I was thinking it might be time for me to tell that story. When are you coming?"

"It depends on my work schedule, but when is best for you?"

"Vanessa, I sit in the same spot each day, waiting for the day to end. If the Lakers are playing, then I wait for that. The last time I checked, my calendar is open."

"Will the weekend after next be okay? I have that weekend off."

"That's fine Vanessa, see you then. Bye."

When the phone clicked, Vanessa hung up the phone, thinking, *damn—same shit different day.* She felt as if a suit of armor was starting to enclose her entire body, protecting her from her Grammy.

Walking away from the phone, Vanessa said aloud to herself, "You better be nice to my babies, or I will put them back in the car and leave Watuppa Grove and never come back."

3

Truth is something you stumble into when you think you're going somewhere else.

—JERRY GARCIA

Dark clouds billowed in from the south and stacked against Sonoma's Mayacamas Mountains, and Maeve began to count down the minutes until school was out. She had been dreading the coming weekend ever since her first-semester conference with her fourth-grade teacher, Mrs. Green. Waiting for the bell to ring, Maeve once again went through the list of equipment she was to bring to her great-grandmother's house. She was dressed in her Girl Scout uniform, and was excited about her meeting after school—a woman from Girl Guides in British Columbia was coming to do an art project with them. But her worry about her interview with her Grammy kept gnawing at her. She glanced at her tennis shoe, teal and tattered, and began to tap her foot, her fingers twirling in her Irish ginger curls.

Mrs. Green's voice climbed above the class to be heard. "Okay, children, you have ten minutes. Let's finish up and pass your papers in. Don't forget to put your names on them."

"Maeve, are you going to Dayanara's birthday party tomorrow?" her friend Sophie asked. "We're going to ride horses in her grandfather's vineyard."

Maeve stopped tapping her foot. "I had hoped to go to the party, but I'm interviewing my Grammy for my Gold Rush project and this is the only weekend we can go. The interview sounded like fun at first but now I'm kind of scared."

"She's your family, Maeve, how hard can it be?"

"She's 98 years old, I hardly ever see her, and besides, I think even my mom is afraid of her. When I was in kindergarten, she came to the Thanksgiving feast and complained to the teacher that dressing the children as Indians was degrading. I remember Toby Johnson teased me for weeks."

"Girls?" Mrs. Green interjected. "Are your papers organized to go home?" Her voice rose to address the class, "Children, don't forget, we're reciting our poems next week." Gathering her things, Maeve looked out the window to see the spring wind howling through the old conifers in front of the school. The limbs danced violently in the turbulence. The children stirred with excitement, and Maeve shivered. The wind brought a deep, rolling thunder, and hail fell out of the afternoon sky in torrents, right as the dismissal bell rang. The children rushed out to the playground, getting drenched and trying to catch the hail in their mouths. Maeve found her younger brother, Brodie, on the playground, soaked and wild-eyed.

"Brodie, you're soaked and we have to go. Mom is waiting for us."

Brodie, playing chase with his friend, ignored her.

Maeve shouted over the sound of the storm, "Mom is going to be really angry with you," as she turned into the hallway to find her mother. Speaking through her teeth with a forced restraint, Maeve shook her head, saying, "Boys."

Suddenly, in a blur, Brodie streaked passed her in the hallway, yelling, "Now Mom is waiting on you, tortoise girl!"

That evening, after putting Maeve and Brodie to bed, Vanessa's memory drifted back to her childhood with her Grammy at Watuppa Grove. Grammy would say, "Chickabiddy, have I told you how much I love you today?"

Vanessa thought, *Grammy used to call me the spunk of the family. What happened? What did I do?* But she knew her Grammy was as unpredictable as the weather, and she wondered how the weather would be when they arrived at Watuppa Grove the next day.

As the children slept, her mind continued to meander to her childhood, and the trips she took with her grandmother and her cousin Emily. Vanessa's mind quickly jumped to the memory of the accident, over a decade ago.

It was a strikingly beautiful day, falling into a new season. After the family Sunday dinner, Vanessa left to join her friends at the theater to see *A Christmas Carol,* despite her family's persistent teasing to join them all in playing dominoes at the Elk's Club. Driving away in her 1965 Volvo, she almost changed her mind, remembering playing dominoes with Grammy Frances. "Think of doubles, chickabiddy," Grammy would proclaim.

It was the twenty-first day of December, the Solstice, teetering between the darkness and light. That was the first year the family did not visit Grammy and Watuppa Grove for Christmas.

Vanessa's cat, Mr. Jones, interrupted her thoughts as he bunted against her leg. Her mind rambled, erratic, curving into Grammy. After years of therapy she had learned to recognize there were just some things you could never control or bring back, like her parents, aunt and uncle, and Emily. She had to find her courage to move forward. Ultimately, she had to take the same journeys everyone did, to find what haunts their past.

She stewed upon what tomorrow would bring for her children. *What lasting impressions will Grammy lay before them? And how will I react if Grammy treats Maeve and Brodie badly? And what will Grammy share about the family's past?*

She forced herself to take slower breaths. Her memory traced over time, recalling a time when she and Emily were 10. The girls were at Watuppa Grove, riding horses, and Vanessa asked her cousin how Grammy's great-grandparents had come up with the money to purchase Watuppa Grove.

Emily said, "I overheard my parents once say something about a boulder of solid gold." Then, biting her lip, she quickly retreated. "Vanessa, please don't ever tell anyone I said that."

Vanessa's memory resurfaced into a different time, when the cousins were in their early teens. Grammy had taken them on trips to Seattle, and across the country to New York. One year, Grammy flew them both to Detroit, just so she could drive her new Oldsmobile off the assembly line and drove back to Watuppa Grove.

Her mind then floated back to the Catalina trip and the bird park. The memory brought a sly smile to her lips. Both girls were nine years old and Grammy was bent on seeing this bird park; the only way there was by bus, up a mountain. Emily and Vanessa set off on their own, and they found a wishing well full of coins. Emily had the idea to lean into the well and harvest the coins at the bottom, and as usual, Vanessa went along with it. The girls saw one last fifty-cent piece at the bottom of the well.

They clearly heard Grammy yell, "Girls, we're leaving, let's get moving!"

Vanessa reached down to grab the last coin but fell into the well headfirst, turning a complete somersault, drenching her whole body. The girls ran to the bus, Vanessa's tennis shoes squishing with water. Grammy was waiting at the door of the bus for them.

As Vanessa boarded the bus, Grammy, her eyes furrowed, whispered, "You embarrassing child."

She had a burning image of her and Emily sitting in the back of the bus as it traveled down the hill, with a small stream of water flowing down the center aisle, then down the bus steps and out the door, while she sat, still clutching the fifty-cent piece.

4

What we do does not define who we are.
What defines us is how well we rise after we fall.

—ANONYMOUS

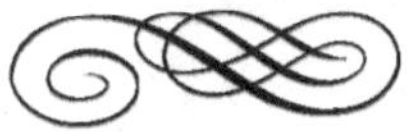

The following morning, Brodie, awake at 5:30, and having slept in his clothes, was up before Maeve, who had not. Brodie sat in his car seat, wrapped in his blanket, his eyelids creased in a sleepy daze, while Vanessa helped her daughter get dressed. Five minutes later, they were off to Watuppa Grove. While her children slept, a forest of almonds blurred, and as Vanessa drove on toward an ominous morning sky and rising sun, her thoughts continued to run through her past. Memories, once locked away in her subconscious, continued to spill out onto the landscape as she focused on the road with its endless row of power lines listing to the north.

After two hours of driving, she rolled out of her reverie and said, "Look, kids, we're here!"

Through the oaks, Brodie could see the majestic rows of Canary Island palm trees leading to Grammy's house. As they made the slow rise up the hill, the house's presence loomed larger than Brodie had remembered. The house had a distinctive vibrancy of color and as Vanessa drove up, she remembered Grammy saying, *"Moutarde de Dijon et d'olive,"* as if its mustard yellow flanked in a olive green trim called out "Here I am" to all those approaching. Six columns rose from the porch and curves of large articulated windows with their fancy brackets and arches blended with widely overhanging cornices and rakes, to the ball and point cupola. It was a wonderful place for a child to play and more memories of her childhood flooded her thoughts.

Maeve and Brodie unlatched their seat belts and were out of the car as soon as their mother secured the emergency brake. "Mom, hurry, open up the back, I need to set up for my interview," Maeve said with clear determination.

Brodie was out of the car and jumped up the stairs two steps at a time, yelling, "Grammy we're here!"

The heavy door swung wide on its solid brass hinges. He found Grammy in the parlor on her red mohair couch reading a book.

She glanced up from her book, looking over her glasses, and said, "Where did you come from? Do I know you?"

Brodie stopped in his tracks, bewildered.

In his most mannered tone, Brodie said, "Grammy, I'm Brodie, you don't remember me? I am your grandson."

"You are too short to be my grandson," she said without looking up from her book.

Brodie climbed up next to her in a snuggle and said, "I knew you would remember me."

Looking down at Brodie, her eyes reflected a joyful light and she said, "Yes, I remember you, little man."

"What are you reading Grammy?"

"The Yale Book of Quotations."

"Why?"

"Quotations are things that real people have said."

"Do you like them?"

"Very much Brodie, they help me ponder the world around me."

"They sound important Grammy."

"To me they are."

Maeve began to unpack her things from the back of the car. "Mom, where is the tripod? I packed it in here yesterday." Her frustration dangled in her voice.

With a long sigh, Vanessa said, "Take a breath, honey, one thing at a time. It's all there, you probably checked it three times yesterday."

"Here it is," continued Maeve as she grabbed the tripod, the camera, and her cassette recorder and began heading up the steps.

Looking up from her book, Grammy watched Maeve through the window, then she glanced back to Brodie over her glasses and noticed he was dressed in Levis, cowboy boots, flannel shirt, with his cowboy hat resting loosely on his head. She said, "Who is this one with all of the equipment? Where did she come from? I like your outfit, by the way."

Confused, Brodie said, while removing his cowboy hat, "Grammy, that's Maeve, my sister...she's a fourth grader and she's here to interview you."

"Why does she want to interview me? I am just an old woman," Grammy said.

"It's for her school project about the Gold Rush."

Maeve and her mother entered with a mound of her stuff in their arms just as Grammy said to Brodie, "Well, I'm not talking to anyone!" while giving a sly smile to Vanessa.

Maeve, stressed, said, "What do you mean you're not talking to anyone?"

"Maeve, can't you say hello to your Grammy?" her mother asked.

"Hi, Grammy, I'm sorry, how are you feeling? Are you ready for my interview?"

"I have decided to not do the interview, sugar pop," she said flatly.

Maeve's eyes, now wide, abruptly welled up, and she looked to her mother for a hanging sliver of hope.

Grammy continued, "But I have decided to do something different." Her eyes glowed like a five-year-old on Christmas morning and the room held its breath for her to speak. Her trembling, arthritic hands slowly set her book on her lap and she spoke. "Children, don't worry, you will get your interview, but not before you complete a small task."

Dumbstruck, Brodie and Maeve looked at each other, with stalled breath, then to their mother, and back to Grammy.

"I am an old, ancient woman who has lived too long. You know," she settled her rickety old frame into the mohair, "this getting old is not for sissies. I have lived in this house my whole life and it is now my prison. I go from the bedroom, to this couch I now sit on, this is my world. So, I have decided to give you two children a small but challenging task."

"What kind of task?" Maeve questioned.

"I suppose you might call it a treasure hunt," she replied, with her eye winking a sparkle to the morning.

With raised eyebrows Brodie asked, "A pirate treasure? I love pirates!"

"The treasure is my story, or perhaps your interview Maeve, I suppose. This is a very old house, over 140 years old, and it holds many stories and secrets. When my great-grandparents built this home, they had a plan. They wanted a home that made some kind of statement about who they were and where they were going. They were adventurers who lived their lives to the fullest. To come to California, for them, was to let go of the past and carve a new future, and this house was their future. Which reminds me of a quote I read the other day: 'The past is solid, and the future is liquid.' I just love that quote. Their new future was the beginning of the new republic of this place called California, and they helped shape its future."

"Mrs. Green, my teacher, has us write a different quote every morning," said Maeve.

"I think I'm going to like your teacher Maeve."

"Grammy?" inquired Brodie. "What about the treasure hunt?"

"Well, yes, the treasure hunt. I knew that I needed a sweet young chickabiddy to keep me on track."

"On track?" Maeve asked.

Grammy explained, "When my great-grandparents had this house built they hired this fancy highfalutin architect, and he liked playful little secrets. They were his signatures so to speak."

Brodie glanced with wrinkled brows at his mother.

"What he liked to do when he built houses, honey," Vanessa explained.

"So," continued Grammy, "when he built this house, he created a few secret passages, which, as a young girl, my brother Harold and I searched and searched for."

"Did you find them, Grammy?" Maeve asked.

"Well, I most certainly did and today it is you and your brother's turn, and if you're successful you will find the treasure!"

"A pirate treasure, Grammy?" Brodie asked, his eyes widening.

A raspy laugh rolled from her throat, and she said, "Yes, little man, a pirate's treasure, or perhaps better yet, a treasure from a pirate."

"Cool," Brodie cooed.

Maeve, ready to move on, said, "Treasure hunts have clues and a map, right?"

"Well, yes they do, Maeve." Looking at Vanessa, Grammy's eyes sparkled. "She's a keeper, this one. When this house was built two secret passages were installed at least that I know of, which both lead to the same place, the treasure place. My game has simple rules you both must ask me yes or no questions. For example, 'Is it in this area of the house?' And I say yes or no. Any questions?"

Vanessa thought, *I don't remember any of this, and I spent a lot of time here, two secret passages? What is going on?* In the moment, what surfaced for her was the clear image of being forced into learning to play the piano and how much she hated it, and when she got really good, her Grammy never asked her to play for her.

"Is it in this room?" asked Maeve.

"No," Grammy said flatly, looking over her glasses.

The children both began asking questions at the same time.

Grammy said, " Hold your horses there, one at a time. Think of places, not rooms."

They took turns blurting out random places. Finally, Maeve suggested the stairs, and Grammy's eyes lit up like blue marbles dancing.

"Getting warm," she said.

Brodie and Maeve bolted from the parlor, to the staircase, and a grand staircase it was. It was the first thing you saw when you came in the front door.

"You must look for a lever that releases a secret door, which leads to a dark passage. Don't be afraid of the dark, as the darkness leads to the light. Here's a hint: my great grandparents loved to read, and loved writing even more." Brodie and Maeve, now fully focused, moved to the small bookcase built into the side of the staircase. Vanessa followed them, leaving Grammy in the parlor alone.

Calling from the other room, Maeve asked, "What are we looking for, once we find the passage?"

"You are looking for a box, a ship captain's box," Grammy said.

"I knew it was a pirate treasure!" Brodie yelped, his eyes wide with excitement.

Vanessa's face flushed, and she said to herself, in her most sarcastic Grammy Frances imitation, which she had practiced over and over front of the mirror, *You are looking for a box, a ship captain's box. Why did she keep this from me?*

Maeve began to run her hands over the bookcase and Brodie followed her lead, touching all of the books. It didn't take long for the children to tire from their Grammy's game. Frustration began to set in, their faces slowly drooping.

Grammy hobbled with her cane into the room with Vanessa and said, "Both of you give up too easily. I spent months and months looking, and I was never given any clues. There will be no quitters in this house. Think, chickabiddies!"

Brodie began pulling books off the lower shelf and quickly realized he was too short to reach the upper shelf. He stacked books on the floor and then stood on them to extend his reach.

Maeve pleaded, "Brodie! Just get a chair, that isn't safe."

After several minutes Brodie lost his balance—quickly he grabbed at the books to balance himself. As he began to fall, the book in his hand pulled away from the shelf and stopped. Brodie crumpled to the floor, his cowboy hat tossed from his head, and suddenly the bookcase magically popped away from the staircase wall. Both children froze, their eyes wide and curious.

With a quick glance Maeve said, "We're going in the bookcase."

As the children disappeared into the bookcase, small batches of blotchy skin bloomed on Vanessa' face. "What is this, Grammy? Why haven't you ever told me this?" Her tone shattered the moment.

While leaning on her cane, Grammy turned and faced Vanessa, her eyes looming beacons over her glasses. "It wasn't your time."

"What is that supposed to mean?"

"What it means is that it was not your time and it is now Maeve and Brodie's time."

Grammy turned and hobbled back to her mohair couch.

Vanessa, now flushed and ready to faint, thought, *Wow, what just happened?*

"Grammy, Mom! Come quick, we found it," said Maeve.

Brodie shouted, "We found it, Grammy! We found it!"

"The stairs are really skinny," said Maeve.

"Yes, I remember them like the back of my hand," responded Grammy. "Let the stairs guide your way."

The space was cramped, even for the children, and they climbed the vintage wooden steps, traveled by few in the last century. The dark, narrow passage did lead, as Grammy had said, to the light of a lone window through the spider webs.

Maeve called out, "Grammy, Mom, we found it, we found a trunk."

Brodie appeared out of the bookcase, his eyes wide and full of the moment. "We found a pirate chest, Mom! It's too big to bring down the stairs."

Grammy interjected, "Not so, young Brodie, that is not so," as Maeve appeared from behind Brodie.

Maeve, her forehead wrinkled, asked, "What do you mean, Grammy?"

"What I mean, chickabiddy, is that box is attached to the floor, so it appears to be stuck there until you figure out how to remove it." Grammy explained, "When the house was built, that box was placed in the passage not to be removed."

"Why?" the children asked in unison as they walked down the stairs to hear more.

"My great grandparents felt that their story was a very special family story and they wanted to keep it in a safe resting place for the family, in this house."

"What if the house burned down?" inquired Maeve.

"Well, there is a secret passage for that as well, sugar pop. I guess they were willing to take that chance. Now you must open the box," Grammy directed.

"How do we do that?" Maeve asked.

"Well, you two need to find the key," said Grammy.

"But pirates don't use a key, Grammy, they shoot the lock off with their muskets."

Laughing with her raspy cough, Grammy said, pointing her twisted arthritic finger at her grandson, "Little man, we have no muskets, but there is one key and both of you must find it." Her eyes widened. "That is, if you wish to find the story, or perhaps your interview."

"How do we do that?" asked Maeve.

Grammy spurted, "Why do you think there is a window up there, chickabiddies?"

Both Brodie and Maeve cast back a blank stare at their Grammy.

Then Brodie, his eyes wide and eager, said to Maeve, " Let's go!" And with that the two adventurers started back up the straw-like stairs, feet pounding into the ancient wood.

"Not so fast, chickabiddies, get back down here," Grammy directed. When the children returned, Grammy drew a long breath and closed her eyes, her hands now folded on the book on her lap. "The box is of mahogany, with brass-bound, military-style bindings, and the handles are counter-sunk, they pull away from the box for you to carry it. Yet this box is unique, it is like a puzzle of secret compartments. That box was the puzzle to end all puzzles for my brother Harold and I. We spent hours and hours and hours trying to get into that box. It was Harold who finally figured out how to open all of the compartments."

"Is that where the pirate treasure is, Grammy?" Brodie quickly responded.

"Yes, little man, a pirate's treasure," Grammy said, with the wink of her eye.

Maeve asked, "What happened to your brother, Grammy?"

"Well, he died in the war. He's buried in France."

"Is that where he died, Grammy?" Brodie probed.

With a quivery smile she said, "Yes, chickabiddy, that is where he died."

5

We discover in others what others hide from us,
and we recognize in others what we hide from ourselves.

—Marquis de Vauvenarques

It was Maeve who found the key in the filtered light of the window, with Grammy directing and Vanessa, from the bookcase, relaying the directions to the children up the narrow passageway. The first step was to use the key to unscrew the box from the floor and bring it down the passageway. Finally, with substantial effort, the box lay on the floor in front of Grammy, Vanessa, and the children as they sat on the red mohair couch. The room filled with the excitement of one hundred Christmas mornings.

Grammy spoke, her voice calling from her raspy throat, "Inside the box are traditional inkwell containers, papers, and toiletry items. There is a lockable box, too. The first set of secret drawers are hidden behind a panel that conceals the secret drawers, which can be released by pressing one of the screws in the brass facing. The box also has a false bottom that can be released by inserting a sharp object into the tiny hole, and hidden drawers." There are a total of six compartments in all.

When the box opened, the children stood next to the box, saturated in awe. One by one, the contents of the box left the darkness and took in the morning light. First, an elegant ivory hand mirror and brush inlayed with mother of pearl.

Maeve said, "Look, Mommy!"

Brodie interjected, "Grammy, is this your great-grandparents' stuff?"

"Yes it is, little mister."

"This is so cool!"

"My goodness, that is the most beautiful pearl necklace I have ever seen," said Vanessa.

Maeve picked up some pearl earrings and a woman's gold ring with a large pearl and said, "This stuff is so pretty, Grammy."

There were two sketchbooks and a handwritten manuscript with a deerskin cover, along with, much to Brodie's excitement, a gold nugget about the size of a Brazil nut.

"I knew it was a pirate treasure, Mom!" Brodie exclaimed, as he held the nugget up to the light.

Vanessa slipped on a ring with a beautiful blue stone.

Maeve picked up a piece of ivory and asked, her brow wrinkled, "What is this?"

Grammy smiled and said, "Why, that looks like a piano key, sugar pop."

"What for?"

"I believe it is for a piano." Grammy glanced at Vanessa with a wry smile.

Brodie opened a small wooden case and discovered a pair of Derringer pistols. Vanessa took them away, and then spotted an antique sewing kit decorated in needlepoint.

In the fifth compartment, Maeve daintily picked up the leather-bound manuscript and asked Grammy, "Is this my interview?"

Grammy winked with a warm smile and said, "If one does not knock on the door, sugar pop, who will answer it?" With that, the kids snuggled into the mohair between their Grammy and their mother. Maeve opened the manuscript and began to read.

6

The vanity of human life is like a river, constantly passing away,
yet constantly coming on.

—ALEXANDER POPE

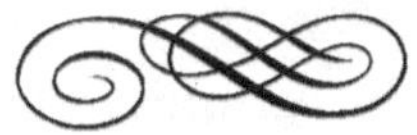

September 9, 1903

To Charlotte, Frances and Harold,

I have wanted to write my memoir for well over half my life. This life journey of mine has been filled with love and sadness. I like to think of them both dancing together in a daring mystical adventure.

My story is but a glimpse of my life from my birth to the summer of 1851. After 70 years of life, I can see that this was a period of tremendous growth and provided the foundation of the woman I have grown to be. Years ago, I decided to wait for the passing of my beloved husband to begin telling the story of the man I loved. Although he often encouraged me, his family held many secrets and we both worried at the ramifications that the story might bring. I have attempted to remember and include the many letters written along with the many conversations and stories that were told to me during this period of my life. I feel fortunate to still be alive to share it with all of you.

I hope to eventually have my story published. Perhaps someone in this family will attempt it, even if it is a hundred years from now.

All my love,

Grammy Claire

September 9, 1830

I joined this world on a clear day in the middle of June, as gnats swirled innocently in the stifling heat. My first fit of wailing was muffled by the deafening screams of my mother, Mary, who lay upon bed sheets lathered in carmine. Her unfortunate passing set the stage for my destiny. My father, Robert, a gentleman of frail demeanor due to his suffering from asthma, fell into a deep depression during the days that followed my mother's death. The death of my mother overwhelmed his soul. After only five days of life, I slept peacefully at my aunt and uncle's home, when my father fell onto an oil lamp, while in a drunken stupor, and died, trapped in his burning house, which lit the night sky with a raging orange glow.

September 9, 1848

I was a bright girl, or so I thought, and received the best of care, which included the finest things life could offer. Being the doted-upon niece of a shipping tycoon, I loved the spotlight and the attention of being a wealthy Bostonian.

At social events other girls would say, "Oh, you have such lovely hair, and your skin looks remarkable, even in the stifling heat." "Where did you get that dress? It is exquisite!"

"It's from Paris," I would answer, bored.

I was being courted by a gentleman named Ashley Stewart, ten years my senior, the prominent son of one of my uncle's business partners. We both appeared, on the surface at least, to be perfect for each other. Both of us had been pampered with the good life, and had a naiveté about the world around us, as if our mere names offered us protection of some sort. Life has a way of making you become your examples.

On this particular morning, I dressed in my newest Delaine dress from Paris, for today I was to receive my new piano. The party dress had a ground weave of a stunning sky blue, with a bright green vine meandering through, bearing yellow berries. The dress fit close at the waist, with a gathered bodice and a full skirt.

I was eager to run my fingers across the keys of ivory and onyx. In anticipation of the piano's arrival, I sat working my newest puzzle, also from Paris. I often fantasized about going to Paris one day, and to perhaps play the piano in a grand hall, as the scent of roses and garden phlox wafted across the lawn and mourning doves cooed in the eaves of the porch with a soothing charm.

A clattering of hooves was coming up the lane and I glanced away from my puzzle to see Levi, who had managed the sprawling five-hundred-acre estate my whole life, approach from the lane with an empty wagon, much to my dismay.

My face pinched, I shouted, "Where is my piano?"

"Still on the docks."

"But why?" My arms were crossed with adolescent scorn.

"It's still in the hold of the ship. The block and tackle sheared and is being repaired. The blacksmith will have it ready perhaps by tomorrow or the day after."

"Well, that just fries my bread!" I stomped my foot upon the porch like a wild horse. "Levi! Get Bluebell ready to ride."

I went to my hatboxes and chose a dark royal blue beveled silk bonnet. How could I ride with prideful honor without a matching bonnet?

The stable and carriage barn was the largest structure on the farm. It sat proudly on the crest of a knoll and overlooked the rest of the estate. Its most unusual exterior feature was the windowed ball and point cupola with six-over-six windows that glanced toward the south. The two-story building had been constructed when I was five years old. My uncle, Jacob McCarthy, was known to take pride in his team of fine horses, which he regularly pranced through the streets of Boston. Jacob had paid attention to detail, and quality was lavished on the construction of the stable, providing a shallow pitched roof and widely overhanging cornices and rakes with vertical bead board siding and flat trim. Double sliding doors provided access to the stables and the interior walls, including the thirty horse stalls, finished in match-stick board. The stalls had custom-worked iron feeders, which were stunning pieces of art.

As I entered the stable, its cool stillness wove a tapestry of smells that brought a calmness and clarity to my life. I glanced upward toward the hayloft, where I'd played as a young girl, swinging on the rope swing for hours with Levi's son, Garland. At that moment, I was overtaken with the image of Garland swinging with me, his laugh both intoxicating and soothing. Slowly my mind filtered through the memory to Garland's death, as he fell into the ice trying to save his new puppy, Buddy. I was ten years old when I stood on the edge of the pond in terror and watched, screaming hopelessly, as Garland began to sink after failing to grab the branch I held out for him. My screams for help did not go unnoticed, and my aunt Amelia, who ran to help us, slipped on the ice, hit her head on some rocks, and died.

Suddenly I found myself back in the silence of the golden tack room, and the morning light glistened, clear and pristine, filling the space in between with the pain of my memory.

****

"What's a tack room?" Brodie asked.

"It's a stable room for storing saddles, harnesses and such. Things you need to care for and ride horses," his mother answered.

"Claire sounds like a spoiled rich girl, Mommy."

"Maeve, I am sure you could use better language to describe Grammy's great- grandmother."

Turning to Vanessa, her eyes beams of light shooting over the rims of her glasses, Grammy said flatly, "Maeve is correct, Claire was a spoiled rich girl, at least at age eighteen."

Vanessa sat, a chill starting to swarm over the length of her spine, and thought, *you will never change, will you, Grammy.*

Vanessa, her voice subdued, said, "Claire's parents, her aunt, and her friend all died, that is awful."

Grammy said, cold and direct, "Death comes to all of us, Vanessa."

7

Destiny stands by sarcastic with our dramatis persona
folded in her hand.

—MARY ANN EVANS

I reached into my tack box for my riding boots while my young dog, Sweet Pea, awaited gratification and bumbled against my feet.

"Stop it!"

As Sweet Pea cowered, I forced on my riding boots with an ornery scorn. I mounted Bluebell and turned her around, my mind still grinding upon the memories of Garland. With a kick of my boots, Bluebell and I sprinted out of the barn, down the lane, and into the woods.

Finally I slowed Bluebell to a primping jaunt, and came to a large spread of toothwort at the edge of the lane. I stared languidly into a backdrop of vibrant green foliage. Bluebell slowed to a stop as cicadas sang from the trees. Entranced, I continued to drift in thought, as if chewing upon the fate of Garland, my aunt, and my piano. I noticed a Paper White butterfly dancing in the air. It circled my head two times and then threaded the air in front of my face, as if in slow motion. I sat there on Bluebell, transfixed by the deep chocolate branch-like markings on the fluttering white wings. Suddenly, my upper lip began to perspire. It was well known that if a Paper White circled your head, romance was in the air, and that made my skin flushed and full. When I was fifteen, I had asked Levi why it meant that romance was coming.

His response to me was, "Because of the butterfly's name, *Pieris virginiensis!*"

I said, "In English, please?"

"Paris Virgin!" Levi said, as he began to laugh deep and full.

I thought, *Just like a man to name a butterfly a Paris Virgin.*

I continued down the lane and turned onto the Boston Post Road. My thoughts turned to Ashley, my ever-absent beau, or so I felt, even though he visited every Saturday and Sunday. The rest of his time he spent working for his father's business. My mind drifted to my hope of him asking for my hand in marriage, and then to the presents he had promised upon his return from New York.

I thought: *Could they be wedding gifts?*

The drone of insects soothed me into a slight reverie as I came to a turn in the road. I encountered a horse tied to a sapling. As I approached, I glanced to the left and fifty yards beyond saw a hat in the brush. *Is it Ashley? Is that a horse from his father's stable?* My eyes quickly scanned the saddlebags.

Why, it is Ashley, I thought. The saddlebags were full with hidden promise. My heart swelled into exhilaration. *It was that pretty Paper White!* My heart raced. *He has brought me gifts,* I thought.

I slid off Bluebell to investigate. Focused on the bags, I approached to open them, carefully watching the hat in the distance turn with a slow elegance. I took a step forward and stepped into a snare, which grabbed my ankle, as the horse spooked and tugged on its rope. The snare hurled me upside down as I gave a startled scream while the sapling of maple snapped sharply with a crispy September twang. The force inverted my world and I saw tumbling hues of celadon blinking. I found myself upside down, in my new Delaine dress with its white lace collar and cuffs, now a tent covering my face. I heard loud, boisterous laughter, which leapt out from the forest.

"Ashley, get me down this instant!"

The laughter continued.

"Ashley, I said now! This is not a laughing matter!"

"Well, you do look rather funny hanging there with those pretty little bloomers of yours," said the stranger.

"Who are you, and what are you doing here?"

"I am Daniel Benet, and I was simply relieving myself after the first leg of my journey to New York. Who is Ashley?" he asked.

"My Ashley is a gentleman, which you are not!" I began to cry.

Daniel said curtly, "Stop that, you're beginning to scare the horses. Calm down and I will cut you loose. Tell me, lady, were you trying to go through my saddlebags? Is that why you are in this snare?"

"I thought that you were Ashley, he is bringing me gifts from New York."

With one quick stroke of his blade, I dropped two feet onto my head, in a disheveled heap, upon the wet earth of September. As I struggled to get up, all I could say was, "Oh, my God, look at my dress," and I continued to cry.

Daniel said, "Let me help you," and gently took my arm.

My eyebrows narrowed into a furrowed row, my voice bouncing into the forest, "Do not touch me!" Resolved, but embarrassed, I turned to face him. My face, hair, and dress were freshly splattered with mud. Daniel once again began to laugh.

My face now flushed and hot, I found myself transfixed by his eyes, which were a piercing shimmer of aquamarine, contrasted against the Atlantic sky, like a dragonfly wing. At this moment, for the first time in my short life, I was speechless. He held out his handkerchief to me, but I did not notice. He stood there and watched me, still with my blue silk bonnet, until I said, "Thank you," and took the handkerchief.

My eyes, I am sure reflected his heartfelt smile with an unknown clarity. As I cleaned the mud from my face, it revealed an Irish flush of exhilaration, flooded with embarrassment, but I continued to maintain my composure.

"I am Benet, Daniel Benet, at your service, madam," he said, and offered his hand with ultimate respect. Suddenly, I found him falling into my pupils, and saw that his stood out like the dot for the letter *i*. Instantly he seemed flushed with a giddy nervousness I had never seen.

The moment, which felt as if it would last forever, surfaced like an upwelling spring lost and forgotten, and then I handed him his handkerchief and said, "Thank you, Mr...."

"Benet, Daniel Benet," he repeated. "You are most welcome." Tipping his hat, he continued, "I am sorry—and you are...?"

With sarcasm dripping like maple sap, I returned, "McCarthy, Claire McCarthy." I turned to mount Bluebell and continued, "Good day, Mr. Benet."

"And also with you, Mrs. Ashley, watch where you step now," he teased, tipping his hat once again. Suddenly my hand darted out and gave a quick slap to his cheek.

My eyebrows rose, my eyes shooting arrows, I said, "How dare you speak to me in such a manner," with that I mounted Bluebell, and turned to face him, my blue eyes full and impudent, as I said smugly, "He is not my husband!" I gave Bluebell a swift kick and rode off.

8

If you do not change direction, you may end up where you are heading.

—GAUTAMA BUDDHA

Daniel stood in the clearing, wiping mud from his face as the sound of hooves faded into the largeness of the forest on the crisp edge of the coming New England fall. With a swelling breath Daniel rallied and thought, *my, what was that all about?*

The crows cawed and swooped at the squirrels, both continuing their ancient quarrel. Daniel mounted his horse and continued on his way. As he rode, the thought of her eyes fixed upon his continued to captivate him, and the thought of her upside down, and then on the ground, her face sprinkled with mud, danced in his mind. He felt that I was absolutely the most beautiful, and possibly the most intriguing woman he had ever laid eyes on.

As he continued his journey down the Boston Post Road, the gait of his mare, Buttons, lulled his thoughts to what awaited him in New York. While mosquitoes droned around him, he pondered his fate as a New Yorker, and his new position as an Apprentice Type Setter at Spears Print Shop, a position arranged by his mother. William Spear was a friend and business partner of her late husband. But as Daniel rode forward, he couldn't keep his mind from wandering back to thoughts of Claire McCarthy. I had had a pronounced effect upon him and I possessed a spirit he had not before experienced.

His naiveté of a large city, of the whole world for that matter, made his arrival in New York one of crowded chaos. After traveling for six days he found New York was a mélange of culture, languages, clothing, and exotic foods he had never experienced. The smells of cooking wafted in the air, tickling his senses. As he rode Buttons through the streets, people looked upon him, strangely transfixed. He eventually realized that he still had a small splattering of mud on his face, which reminded him again of Claire McCarthy.

Daniel decided he would try to find the print shop first and then look for a stable for Buttons. After making many stops, he found William Spear's Print Shop. With no place to tie the horse, he used the handle to the print shop door.

When Daniel entered the shop, Mr. Spear shouted, "Mr. Benet, I presume. This is not a stable. If I am to teach you my trade, I will not house your horse!"

"Absolutely, Mr. Spear. Is there anywhere in New York I can house my horse?"

"The nearest stable is on 147th Street, perhaps place 600 or so."

Daniel was surprised that the stable was actually a brownstone with a ramp, nothing out of the ordinary really, like all of the other houses in the row. It was here that Daniel discovered that the cost of boarding a horse in New York would be most of his daily wages. So he and his dear friend Buttons parted ways. Although Daniel now had fifty dollars more in his pocket, he felt disconnected and forlorn. His new life depended upon the balance of this moment. He wondered about the printing business and Mr. Spear. When he returned to the print shop, worn and tired, Claire McCarthy still dancing in his head, old man Spear handed him directions to Nell's boarding house and said he had made arrangements for him to stay there.

As Daniel turned to leave, Spear barked, "Mr. Benet, this is when a gentleman would say thank you."

As he reached for the door Daniel turned and said, "I'm sorry, Mr. Spear, it has been quite the day, with me getting here and all. Thanks for all you've done."

A slight sheen of sweat percolated on Spear's forehead, his eyes narrowed and impatient, he continued, "Gentlemen, Mr. Benet, do not make excuses for their behavior."

Daniel left and the shop doorbell jingled as it closed.

****

Frowning, Maeve said, "Why is Claire so demanding? She seems so uppity, like everyone owes her something."

"She is just like this girl Christy in my class at school. The boys call her Prissy Christy," Brodie answered.

Shocked by her son's words, Vanessa declared, "Brodie! You don't say those things, ever, not to anyone. That is not how a gentleman acts."

Maeve interjected, "Mrs. Green said that bullying is against the law."

"I don't, Mom, only Nathan and Nathaniel do," Brodie protested.

"Young man, we are not talking about Nathan and Nathaniel, are we?" his mother said sternly.

Grammy added, "My mother taught my brother and me, that you always get more with honey than you do with vinegar."

"Honey with vinegar?" Brodie asked.

"Honey is sweet and vinegar is sour. It means be sweet and nice to everyone, not sour," Mom explained.

Vanessa thought, *perhaps you should have practiced what your mother preached.*

Vanessa's memory drifted back to Watuppa Grove at age sixteen, as she too bolted out of the barn, on her horse, pouting about the news of an afternoon piano lesson. Vanessa asked herself, *I wonder if Claire hated her piano lessons in the beginning?* Then Vanessa thought of Claire meeting Daniel in the forest. She remembered the exact moment she met Liam, Maeve and Brodie's father. His eyes, those piercing blue eyes, swallowing her into a landscape she had never experienced.

Thoughts of Liam left her hungry and alone. He was scheduled to arrive home in ninety-three days, after eight months on assignment for a high-level government agency. Vanessa never really knew where he was until he got home.

Grammy began to read again, her voice a weathered stone, cracked and ancient. Her breath searched for punctuation. Grammy's rhythmic demarcation slowly pulled Vanessa back into Claire's story.

9

I am plus my circumstances.

—JOSE ORTEGA Y GASSET

I rode Bluebell hard and fast, with the encounter of Daniel Benet and the Paper White butterfly filling my mind. What an uncanny tone the encounter had left upon me.

What was it about him? His eyes were like the soul of an untamed past lingering on the surface of my skin.

When I returned to Watuppa Pond, I found Levi cleaning the stalls, waiting for me.

"Miss Claire, it appears you have fallen off your horse, are you hurt?"

"No, I am not, but as you can see I have ruined my new dress."

"Yes, I can see that." Levi's eyes sought answers. "Yet there is something else, what is it?" Levi knew me better than anyone and could read me like a day-old trail.

I began to head back to the house, turning to Levi. "It's nothing. Please rub down Bluebell well, I gave her a hard ride." With that, I sauntered toward the house with a roused gait.

Watching me walk away, Levi must have wondered what secret I was holding onto now.

The following day Ashley finally returned from New York, carrying gifts of crystal and silver, along with assorted linens and trinkets. I responded with a sugarcoated curtsy. Ashley spoke about his trip to New York, with a rasp in his voice. Once again, he had developed a bad cough.

"Are you feeling well, Ashley? What is wrong?"

"It's just the city air, I suspect. I have a proposition for you, can you please sit down."

I sat on a French Rococo parlor chair as my heart swelled with the hope of a marriage proposal.

"My uncle's business has procured a mail contract from the United States Government, and is launching a new venture to deliver mail to South America and around the horn to California. He has asked me to represent the company in negotiations in South America and California. He thinks it will be good for my health."

"What are you saying Ashley? You are leaving?"

"I am saying I want you to come with me."

"So you are asking my hand in marriage?" I paused, frowning. "It would be dishonorable to accompany you anywhere as an unmarried woman. I will not be cast as your whore mistress." I turned and sighed a deep pout, glancing through the windows at the juncos busily hopping in the tree limbs off the porch.

"Of course, my dear Claire. Will you marry me?"

"Taking your hand in marriage is one thing, following you halfway around the world is quite another. What about my uncle, Watuppa Pond, and my new piano?"

"These are items we must discuss further, Claire."

"And just when does this insipid journey begin?"

"The mail ship *California* departs from New York on October 6."

"That is no time for a proper marriage! What would people think? I will tell you what they will think, that I am a whore and pregnant. I will not accept this preposterous proposal of yours."

"My Claire, you are no whore, and we both know you are not pregnant. We are in love, what is to matter? I can make the arrangements for a grand ceremony with all of the class, distinction, and respect that you deserve." Ashley drew his handkerchief and coughed hoarsely into it, then folded it into his pocket. "The mere suddenness of these business events will explain everything, I assure you. My father says the warm weather will be good for both of us. Marry me, Claire, come with me, on our grand adventure toward our future."

Finally, my face now relaxing with intent, I responded, "I will accept this absurd proposal of yours under two conditions."

Ashley tilted his head, wondering what the request would be. "Yes?"

"We shall have the proper wedding that I deserve and—"

"And?" he asked.

"My new piano comes with me," I answered with a cultured authority.

With wide eyes, his eyebrows reaching up to his forehead, he pleaded, "My God, Claire, what kind of request is that?"

I coyly responded, "Simply put, my dear, that kind of request is mine."

"So then I have preparations to administer." He leaned to kiss my cheek. "Good day, my dear."

As he left, I heard him mumble, "I can just hear my father. She plans on bringing her piano? My God!"

Still sitting in the French Rococo parlor chair, I began to feel as if I might now be finally complete.

10

I got my wish— the wedding I felt I deserved and then some. Ashley and I were in a massive rush to organize our lives for our great adventure. My uncle was furious about the piano, but as usual, anything I asked for I received. I dressed in my finest, including a hat and sun umbrella. The carriage cracked the ice of a New England fall as it clamored down the lane. Levi had the wagon stocked full of our things, as we, the newlyweds, rode ahead in the carriage.

"Ashley, did you remember to hire someone to tune my piano once it is in place?"

With a sigh he responded, "Yes, my sweet Claire, and he will also return your carriage with Levi."

As the chill of the coming winter crusted our coach, and leaves danced in the wind, Levi accompanied Ashley and me to New York as man and wife.

When we stepped off onto the dock, Ashley and I marveled at the lines of the *California,* which emulated some of the most magnificent clipper ships ever made. With a gleaming black hull, red paddle wheels, white upper works, and plenty of polished brass, the

California was a striking image against the blue water. Her elegant lines were beautiful, built of choice oak and cedar. Her hull was reinforced with diagonal iron straps to stabilize the pounding of her paddle wheels. She was rigged with three masts and a full suit of sails. The wind was meant to be only an auxiliary source of power; she was expected to carry a full head of steam at all times.

"Ashley, how long will we be trapped on this ship?"

"Perhaps three or four months, dear."

Upon seeing the cramped quarters, my face drooped and I said, "You said that we were going on an adventure, but this appears a prison sentence."

"Now, Claire, we must stay positive."

"Ashley, what on Earth shall I do for three months?"

"Well, for starters, you have brought your piano, books, puzzles, and journal. You have always said you wanted to write poetry and draw. There is also one other thing you have, my sweet bride."

With dripping sarcasm I retorted, "Which is?"

With a sly smile and a wink of his eye, Ashley declared, "Why, me, Claire, your loving husband."

"Oh, Ashley, you are such a huckleberry." I melted into his shoulder, my entire body tingling with warmth.

11

Why not go out on a limb, isn't that where the fruit is?

—FRANK SCULLY

December 1848

The sky loomed ominously in hues of mauve and crimson, and in the fading light the winter wind whipped Daniel Benet's hair. Braced against the gusts, heading down Howard Street, away from Spear's Print Shop. Spear had humiliated him once again, and for the very last time. Daniel was finished with Spear, with his rudeness and arrogance. He was a downright nasty, horrible man. The thought of Spear scolding him, in front of Horace Greely, a man Daniel admired, and because of Spear's own negligence. The day left a foul taste lingering in Daniel's thoughts.

Spear was unaware of Daniel's intentions. In his mind's eye, he reveled in Spear's future dismay. But after almost three months of working with the sharp-tongued bully, Daniel had had enough. He had no idea what he would do, but was comforted knowing he would no longer smell of ink and chemicals. His stride, almost skipping over the cobblestones, brandished a brash flush of personal power. The mere thought of old man Spear's plight left him exhilarated and eager. He would not spend another day with him. As the sky drew its curtain of night, he heard the muffled sounds of an altercation. He squinted into the awaiting darkness, and saw three figures emerge from the shadows. Two men were roughing up the third pretty bad.

"Hey! Leave him be!" Daniel shouted.

The men continued to kick and hit the man, ignoring him. Daniel picked up a board to threaten the men, which they ignored in their drunken stupor. Gripping the board tightly, Daniel swung hard, striking one of the muggers across his shoulder blade with such force that he was knocked off the victim. His companion lunged for Daniel and managed to swing at him, but missed.

The other man said, "Piss off, cracka, he deserved it." He helped his friend to his feet and they ran into the coming night, now mottled in shaded tones. In the shadows of the alleyway, the battered man laid motionless.

"Hey, my friend, they've gone, are you hurt bad?"

Slowly the victim's eyes opened into the fading light, full of fear and helplessness.

"What's your name?"

He grabbed Daniel's coat with his hands, pulling him close, his voice garbled and liquored, and his lungs rasped for the slightest breath.

"I, I am—Samuel Fairagain…. The blokes have cut me….cut me deep, they did." His eyes of cobalt searched Daniel's face, and he began to cough up blood.

In a strained but determined voice the man said, "Take my tic—"

"Take your what?" Daniel asked, fearful, his eyes tilted like moons.

"In my pocket…take it."

The man's clenched fists retracted from Daniel's coat and fell back, dead. Daniel looked around for help, but saw no one, and was overtaken with the thought of being accused as the killer. Suddenly, an upwelling of fear danced before him, his face growing hot and flushed. His trembling fingers gently searched the man's clothing, and there, in his pocket, was an envelope. After quickly searching the alleyway, he grabbed the envelope and ran, leaving the man in the shadows.

Back in his room at Nell's boarding house, he took a chest full of air, and he held it as if it was his last. He reflected upon the dark dankness of his room, in the flickering light of a candle dancing, the smoke hovering above him. Daniel's mind drifted to his mother's home, filled with repose and agony. Images surfaced that reflected, sharp and clear, the events of his father's death. That sadness emanated through the layers of discontent in his life. He thought of his father's hopes and dreams—to go to California, "God's country," he called it. He clutched the faded envelope with trembling hands and, drawing an anxious breath, he opened it.

Inside, he discovered a ticket for the steamship *SS Falcon*, to Chagres, New Granada, and continuing on to California on the steamship *SS California*. Also, the envelope contained $800.00 in City Bank Notes.

He emitted a silent, wild howl, as the moment hit him like a bucking horse, full of bluster and unanswered certainty. As his mind reeled from the events of the evening, a wrestling fatigue encompassed his presence. He thought, *California, my lord! I might as well try to fly like a bird.* The ticket clearly stated one-way passage to the Isthmus of Panama, then portage to Panama City, and then on to California. The steamship *SS Falcon* left at noon the next day.

He pondered his situation. His mother, whom he had not seen in three years, his courted lady friend, Anna, back in Boston, their hopes and possibilities. Daniel Benet was now presented with a dilemma, full of danger and hope. California had somehow fallen into his life, by chance and circumstance. He thought, *how could I pass on such a simple twist of fate? Or perhaps it is destiny?*

After a few whiskeys, he found that going to California made sense. In a numbed voice, he spoke to himself, "I now have no employment, over eleven hundred dollars, and a ticket to California." His gaze drifted into the bouncing candlelight and he thought, *Land is what I hoped for, what my father before me hoped for, and in California it will be free for the taking. The people who loved him would still love him, they would support this serendipitous fate laid before him. Who was this Samuel Fairagain, just how did he come to have passage to California and how was it that he was now dead? Was he traveling alone? Would he be expected to board the steamship with a traveling partner?* Weighing his thoughts, Daniel Benet began drunkenly to organize his things and prepare for warmer weather.

12

Perhaps the truth depends on a walk around the lake.

—WALLACE STEVENS

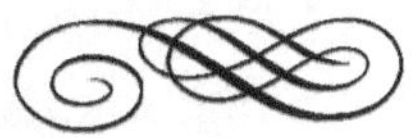

With glee, Brodie said, "This is a pirate story, isn't it, Grammy. I just knew it! When's lunch, Mom?"

Before Vanessa could respond, her grandmother looked up from the book and announced, "Leah has prepared us a feast of soup and grilled cheese sandwiches."

"Who is Leah?" the children asked.

"She is my attendant."

"Your what?" Brodie asked.

"She helps me move about, she cooks and cleans—you know, that kind of stuff."

"Where did she come from?"

"Brodie, you don't ask those questions," his mother interjected.

"Why not, Mom?"

Grammy continued, "Well, little man, if you need to know, she came from Uganda." She pushed a small button on her wristband.

"Uganda, where is that?"

"Uganda is in Africa, honey," Vanessa answered.

"It's the continent that looks like a horse's head," Maeve proudly declared. "I learned that from Mrs. Green."

Leah appeared, wearing light blue capri pants and a peach tee with 3/4 sleeves, against skin of warm milk chocolate. In perfect English with a strong British accent, she asked, "Are you ready for lunch, Frances?"

"Yes, please, Leah, that would be nice. Leah, I'd like you to meet my granddaughter, Vanessa, and her lovely children, Maeve and Brodie. My only great-grandchildren."

Her face was fresh and inviting, and with soft eyes and said, "Nice to meet you. Frances has told me so much about all of you. Welcome back to Watuppa Grove."

After Leah left for the kitchen, Brodie, now squinting, asked, "Are you sure she's from Africa? She sounds like Mrs. Ford at school, but she's from England."

"Honey, Uganda was once ruled by England, and English is taught in the schools there," his mother replied.

Vanessa fell back into her thoughts. *She told you so much about us? Like what?*

13

The world stands aside to let anyone pass who knows where he is going.

—DAVID STAR JORDAN

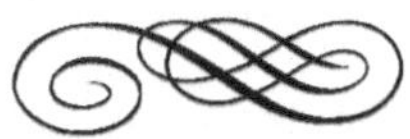

Daniel awoke with a start. The darkness of morning yielded to the light and clung to the chill. His mind still reeled from the chaos of the previous evening, but he grabbed his hat and clothes, his sketchbook and journal, his ink and pens, his father's knife, dragoon, and the little ammunition he had, and left without looking back.

As Daniel approached the dock, he was focused with intent, as the light from the east dawned a new day. The *SS Falcon* of his destiny lay before him. Daniel pondered his next move. He wondered if his best boarding strategy would be to tell the truth, to allow his fate to drift to the four winds and hold fast. He stood among the crates on the dock and watched for some kind of signal. The wharf was speckled with spectators, investors, stevedores, and dockworkers, no doubt saying goodbye and hoping for a safe passage. There was a boisterous feeling of glamor, excitement, and adventure, along with a fragile sense that mayhem beckoned from the shadows. A mangy dog wandered the wharf, begging for a meal as a scrappy cat carrying a wharf rat in its mouth ran ahead. He needed more time to ground himself with a plan and strengthen his nerves.

Daniel Benet's ticket was for the now-departed Samuel Fairagain, a man of Welsh descent, age 33. Daniel would not be that age in a decade. How could he lie?

Just then a gentleman, a woman, and what looked to be the woman's attendant approached the dock to board, and Daniel heard the boarding attendant say, "Is Mr. Fairagain accompanying you?"

The gentleman interjected, "My goodness, I had hoped he boarded already."

"Your party is in cabins 13, 14, and 15, welcome to the *Falcon*. Sir, madam, can I please take your bags?"

"Yes, of course," they responded.

The *Falcon* swayed upon her moorings as if eagerly awaiting something hidden, yet promising, and heavy swells rolled in from the point at Sandy Hook. With his nerves churning in his stomach, Daniel assembled his courage and finally made his move toward the boarding area.

"Good day, sir."

"Yes, it is a good day to sail, Mr...." said the Negro porter, who was dressed in green mohair suit and top hat.

"Fairagain, Samuel Fairagain."

"Welcome aboard, Mr. Fairagain, the governor is awaiting you in his cabin, number 15."

As Daniel boarded the ship, a shroud of tingling numbness slithered around his neck. His face flushed in the morning chill. He approached cabin 15, and a woman's voice echoed back at him. With a sharp step toward his destiny, Daniel Benet knocked on the door of cabin 15. As the door swung open, a large man, stout and burly, filled his frame of vision, with eyes like ink spots of indigo.

"Yes?" he said.

"Good morning, sir," Daniel held out his hand in greeting. "Benet, Daniel Benet, also known as Samuel Fairagain."

"What kind of joke is this?"

"It's not a joke, sir, but a very sad tale. May I explain?"

With disdain, he glanced to his wife, and then back to Daniel, "I presume you must. We can go to the saloon for a drink."

The governor ordered a whiskey and Daniel a beer. They reclined upon the deck in chairs of freshly milled mahogany, as storm clouds loomed dark and ominous, ready to spill the heavens.

"So, Mr. Benet, why are you using my assistant's name and ticket?"

"I have all of his money as well."

"I see. And you procured his property how?"

Daniel began, "I was walking home at dusk last night. I had just quit my job and I was admiring the sky, as it was wild and large with color, when I heard a ruckus as I came upon an alleyway. There were two men beating a man and I broke it up and chased them off, but unfortunately I was too late. They had stabbed him deep. As he lay dying he told me to take his ticket and money for his grand adventure."

Governor Persifor Smith stared at him, then out at the harbor.

Searching, Daniel questioned, "Sir?" Hoping for a reaction, and receiving none, he continued, "He died in my arms and I am now here."

Staring out toward Sandy Hook, the governor said, "Goddamn you, Samuel! Christ almighty. You drunken, gambling son of a bitch."

After a long pause and a swift tip of his whisky, the governor then called for another. The newly appointed Military Governor of California cast a piercing gaze upon the horizon. The sea churned as thunderbolts illuminated the water in the casting darkness of the coming storm.

Finally Smith said, "He was my friend, my confidant, my adviser, and the jackass on my shoulder."

"I am so sorry, sir."

"He was of a peculiar persuasion, you know, and that worried me," the governor returned.

"How so, if I may ask, sir?"

"Let's say he was just of a different sort, son. Samuel looked at the world through a different side of the prism than everyone else." Throwing back the last of his second whiskey, the governor continued, "Well, Benet, since you are here, you are now my new assistant. Can you please bring my wife and I some tea? You should also get settled into your cabin before this weather hits."

Ancient clouds stacked against the afternoon sky and rain fell in torrents in the distance, with the horizon retreating to the color of bruised fruit. Beyond, in the distance, lightning forked across the water and the tumultuous seas began to churn under the bowels of the *Falcon*.

The following morning, the sky jumped out large and blue, and by late afternoon passengers lounged, many with their feet hanging over the sides of the steamer and began to meet one another. There were a mélange of passengers on the *Falcon,* several officers of the Navy, who were educated and possessed steadiness and purpose, some traveling with their wives. There were pompous New England merchants, who lulled on the deck with their penetrating, narcissistic faces, smoking their cigars with a whiskey back, bragging about their accomplishments. Perhaps what they hoped for was an adventure, yet soon they realized travel, for them, would be an uncomfortable business, being trapped and sequestered to a ship, cramped with intrusive elements. There were the Irish, English, and Germans whose precise character was clear and apparent upon their faces of genuine spirit, each flanked by their personal histories. The missionaries, perched on the cross of Jesus, were fervent to transform natives into civilization and lay ground for hope and God.

The *Falcon* moored off the coast of Chesapeake Bay, awaiting a mail delivery, and the passengers lounged in the slowness, saturated in the warmth of a winter day on calm water. The governor and his wife were stoic companions, asking for little but tea and information from the day. Daniel had struck a particular acquaintance with Mr. Kent, who dreamed of being an actor. He was fatherly yet personable, and a comically animated sort of chap. He told vivid tales of his travels and those of his lovely wife, along with their dream of owning land in paradise, a place called California.

14

In each of us there is a little of the rest of us.

—ANONYMOUS

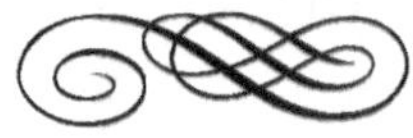

December 5, 1848

Dearest Uncle,

I have been on this wretched boat for four weeks and have grown weary of its quarters, the food, and the company. There are five preachers on the voyage so there is no shortage of the good word. They have even organized a Bible study group, which reflects on one passage a day. The only thing that is positive is the weather, which has been absolutely gorgeous. The *California* is a beautiful ship made with the finest woods and with fine lines of design, yet there is no privacy, especially in regards to the privy. Ashley has been vacant toward me, as he is fully engaged with the ship and the other men. I feel as though I might as well be marooned on a desert island. I have been reading and working on my puzzles to stay occupied, as well as writing poetry. My piano has been secured to the stateroom floor and has been a genuine release for myself as well as the passengers.

They appear to enjoy my playing and several musicians have joined in. It has been a delightful and fun respite from the cramped conditions. Please send my best to Levi.

Fondly,

Claire

15

Friendship improves happiness, and abates misery,
by doubling our joys, and dividing our grief.

—Marcus Tullius Cicero

A cloudless sky painted the horizon as the *Falcon* moved farther down the coast. The weather became ever more nourishing, soothing the abrasive bite of winter for all aboard, as they lounged toward hope upon the deck. Each afternoon, the governor, Daniel, Mr. Kent, and several military men, with their stout faces, and their perceptive and clear affect, played dominoes, sharing stories of their adventures and smoking cigars. It was a peaceful and relaxing time for Daniel, since male comrades had been absent in his life after his father's passing. The men teased him, the youngest of the group, into telling his story. The story that surfaced was that of Daniel and I. All of the men laughed big and large at his telling, which puzzled him somewhat.

Daniel asked, "What's so funny?"

They said, "Why are you on this boat, boy?"

Finally, the governor leaned toward Daniel, withdrew the cigar from his mouth, and said, "Benet, certain predicaments or events that unfold in your life are like doors to a twist of fate. My mother used to say, 'Persifor, if you do not knock on the door, who will ever open it for you?'"

This manner of speaking was new to Daniel, and as he began to play his hand he savored their words.

The days on the steamer unfolded leisurely, the sea gathering calm and fresh. After mail stops in Charleston and Savannah, the *Falcon* headed into Havana Bay. The days lingered in warmth, with the presence of good weather and community. The water swirled in mottled colors of turquoise, which permeated toward the horizon. The pleasant weather, for Daniel, a New Englander, was a soothing companion. The food was marginal at best, in fact largely awful, but the drink and camaraderie filled his soul. As the *Falcon* approached Havana, it was met with a tropical lusciousness that Daniel had never before experienced. He saw forests of emerald, and palms swayed against the Cuban sky, dancing a perfect ballet in the Caribbean winter breeze. He sketched it all.

The *Falcon* moored off the harbor, as tiled roofs and adobe awaited the crew and passengers. The travelers could not explore this newfound paradise, because cholera had broken out in New York and all passengers were sequestered to the boat. All on board longed to rid their legs of the sea, but for two days the *Falcon* sat tethered to the bay while the breeze swayed the palms in a seductive dance.

To reciprocate the ones given to them, Daniel and Mr. Kent purchased a box of cigars from a boy of about twelve, selling his wares from an old rickety boat. The travelers then discovered that the *Falcon* was now laden with exotic fruits and kegs of rum and fresh beer. They felt renewed and fresh; even though they'd never set foot upon the Isle of Cuba, they were lulled and content as they sailed toward New Orleans.

Three days later the *Falcon* arrived in New Orleans to a riotous crowd on the docks. There were many questions as to why, yet as the *Falcon* approached the dock, they saw men with faces of a frenzied storm coming off the gulf. Intemperate men with guns and wads of money in their hands waved them at the ship, shouting as it got closer to the dock. At this moment, everyone on the ship now understood, gold had been discovered in California and they wanted their passage. Everyone chose to stay on the ship in fear that they could not get back on. All on board watched the theater on the docks, while men pressed vehemently to board the skiff to the *Falcon*. After the men boarded, the entire mood of the ship changed to one of a compressive anxiousness. Daniel's group continued to play dominoes on the deck, which was now shared with the Argonauts, who spent most of their time drinking, smoking, and shooting dolphins, as if it were a sport of target practice.

A young gentleman approached the game carrying a locked box and said, "I have never heard so many rude, foul-mouthed men in one place. Mind if I join you?" The players pondered his request, as eyes glanced about for a group answer.

Then the governor's voice danced a gentlemanly tone and said, "We would be honored for you to join us young man," and then, in an abrupt voice, "Benet, your play!" The young man placed his box onto the deck next to Daniel and sat on it.

As introductions circled through the group, Daniel pondered his next move.

The governor's voice ruptured his thoughts: "And here we have Benet, Daniel Benet of Boston. He's someone who has an interesting story and we're going to get it out of him, possibly with your help."

The newcomer looked at Daniel and said, *"C'est un plaisir de vous rencontrer Monsieur Benet, Daniel Benet. Je suis Galvez, Philippe Galvez. Vous êtes Français? Vous avez un nom Français."*

The look on Daniel's face was obvious to the governor and Mr. Kent, and they yanked at their cigars and laughed.

Kent said, "Why, my Grammy used to say, you be just like two peas in a pod. He just told you, it's a pleasure to meet you Mr. Benet,

Daniel Benet. He wants to know if you are French. He said your name is French."

"I do not speak French, but yes, Benet is French."

The laughter continued as Daniel contemplated his play.

The governor leaned into him and said, "Take no offense here, son, we're just funning you."

After playing his hand, Daniel posed a question to the group. "These men that boarded in New Orleans, was it luck or fate that brought them here?"

"Perhaps both," answered Philippe. "They are fevered with the lust for gold. I procured my passage only yesterday. I found out about the gold being discovered in California when I arrived at the docks."

The governor asked, "So what exactly are you running away from, Mr. Galvez?"

Philippe's eyes wandered starboard for a short moment, then he returned his gaze to the governor and said, "I am not running from anything, merely traveling toward my future."

"Which is?"

"Which is yet to be discovered."

The governor chuckled and said, "Perhaps you should turn that question to your own predicament, young Daniel. Is it luck or fate as to why you are here?"

Although it was simply good-natured banter, Daniel was flushed with the moment.

The governor again leaned toward him, his eyes sea green and lathered with time, and said, "Sometimes it is luck, but usually it's just keeping your eyes open."

Another man slowly approached the game, obviously intoxicated; he held tightly to the rail, to steady himself, and asked, "My name is Frederick, what are you fine chaps playing?"

All in the group responded, "Dominoes," without looking up.

The man realized he was being ignored, and shouted over the group, "Piss off then, you crazy crackas," as he cautiously began to move starboard.

"What an ass of a man," said Daniel.

Mr. Kent interjected in his Shakespearean tone, "It is not what men put into their mouth, but perhaps, all of the things which come out of their mouths."

At this moment, the man leaned over the rail with raised hands and said, "I carry the weight of God," and vomited into the wind, which painted the front of his face and shirt.

The temperament of the Argonauts was distasteful, as were the overcrowding and overwhelming stench. After almost two weeks at sea, the *Falcon* approached Chagres, as hope and promise ignited amongst the travelers.

16

*The only real voyage of discovery consists
not in seeking new landscapes but in having new eyes.*

—MARCEL PROUST

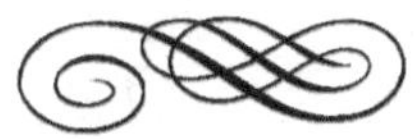

January 5, 1849
Dearest Mother,

By some mystery of fate, I came upon a circumstance that allowed me to travel to California. I am now aboard the steamship *SS Falcon,* heading to Chagres, New Granada. I will then travel the fifty miles across the Isthmus to board the steamship *SS California* to San Francisco.

There are days that seem endless. I have been writing in my journal and I sketch daily. I have taken companionship with several gentlemen, all but one much older than I. One, a Mr. Kent, I admire the most. He is quite the storyteller and an excellent player of dominoes. He also has an affection for cigars, which has grown on me as well, for we together have bought a box of one hundred during our short stay in Havana, Cuba. We were not allowed to board the island due to the cholera epidemic in New York. I hope that you enjoy my sketch of Cuba!

When we reached New Orleans, we found out that gold had been discovered in California, as 500 drunken and riotous men wanted to board the ship. The ones who made it on board are the most despicable creatures I have ever seen. With the exception of one gentleman I met, Philippe Galvez, who is of my age and stature. He has joined our domino game and the older men tease us both about being brothers, as we resemble each other in several ways. Most days we keep to our group and play our games. I have never encountered so many ill-mannered fellows in one place. I pray for my safety and my belongings. Give my love to all.

Fondly,

Daniel

17

Fate rules the affairs of mankind in no recognizable order.

—SENECA

Philippe Galvez was a man with a past not easy to mention. His parents, their love and compassion for each other and for those whom they loved, lived life with enthusiasm and with all the power and wealth that this enthusiasm granted. Philippe was born on a Texas island compound, which was the property of his father. His family had to escape from their island home because of conflicts with nature and government, as his father was a privateer. There were those who said he was a criminal, but most claimed he was a pirate. Because of this, for his safety, Philippe was named after the island of his birth, not his father.

As a baby, Philippe landed in New Orleans with his mother, who raised him in a converted stable, which became an inn. The whereabouts of his father were a mystery. This day at the age of twenty-four, Philippe found himself north of Baton Rouge on the Chretien Point Plantation. During the War of 1812, a kindred friendship between Philippe's father, his uncle, and a man named Hippolyte Chretian grew among the three French compatriots. All Philippe knew was that his father was a business associate of Hippolyte and his Spanish wife, Felicite. When Philippe arrived, Hippolyte had died of Yellow

Fever years earlier, but he found the plantation being run quite smoothly by his widow, Felicite. She was a spirited woman whose behavior was quite unconventional for her time. She was active in the management of the plantation business, smoked cigars, drank whiskey, and was a very good card player. She stood up to any man or beast. She rode a horse like a man and increased the plantation holdings by whatever methods she could. Fortunately for Philippe, she treated him fairly, but she would put him or anyone else in their place if needed. It was honest enough work, with the exception of how the slaves were treated. Philippe thought it was wrong to treat humans so heinously. Most folks treated their hogs better.

It was nearing the end of November, and Philippe was searching for lost stock, as an early snow gathered on his hat and shoulders. He was cold and tired as his horse, Henry, lumbered through the freshly fallen snow. As he rode, his thoughts drifted to his future. The plantation was not going anywhere and things had to change. Suddenly Henry stopped, and began to nibble a patch of grass that poked out from the snow. In the distance, Philippe heard a woman's scream, a moment later another. He prodded Henry to pick up his pace and as he neared the sound of men talking, stopped and tied Henry to a tree. Philippe grabbed his rifle and cartridges and checked his dragoon on his hip, then cautiously walked toward the sound as another scream filled the forest. Philippe came upon the trio, two men and a woman: a mulatto slave, and the men, slave hunters. The men, one short and lean with a pockmarked face, and the other large with a round belly and a vacant affect, had tied the woman to a hickory and beaten her.

Her blood was spattered upon newly fallen snow and her clothes were ripped. "Listen to me, you Negro wench!" said the short man as the larger one hit her across her face with the back of his hand, blood spraying to her right.

"You tell me, who's your master?" said the short man, and he continued, "Negro wench."

The woman, now wailing, pleaded that she had no master. She was a free woman.

He grabbed her hair and yanked her head, forcing her to look at him.

The smaller man said to his accomplice, "Get her ready." In seconds her clothes were being pulled, and snow immediately began collecting upon her bronze skin.

A pistol shot shouted into the silence as Philippe steadied his aim, with his rifle loaded in a notch in a tree. "Hold on there, boys, move and you're dead," barked Philippe, as he readied for reloading.

The shorter man grabbed for his pistol as the rifle cracked an echo across the glen. The man exploded backward and landed on his back. The large man began to bolt for his horse, his long legs kicking up the powder as another shot consumed the silence and hit the man in the back of the head. The white background now blurred with blood, as the man fell face-first into the snow.

"Please don't hurt me," begged the woman, shivering from the crisp air on her skin, bloodied and bruised. Her left eye was swollen closed, with a gash along her brow line. With one quick whip of his knife the woman was free, falling to the frozen ground in a heap. Philippe wrapped her in a blanket and carried her to a horse, tying her into the saddle, as the woman sank into unconsciousness. Philippe quickly searched the saddlebags and found cornmeal and salt pork, a canteen and a blanket. He left the men where they lay, in the glen under the big hickory. Philippe let the second horse free and slapped her hard and she bolted out into the forest. He tied the other horse to Henry and left as the snow began to fall thick and wet. He thought: *just what we need, just keep falling and hide our trail.*

18

Life is either a daring adventure or nothing at all.

—HELEN KELLER

When the *Falcon* arrived in Chagres, it was not able to anchor near the town. At the mouth of the Chagres River were reefs and sandbars, which prevented the deep-hulled ships from entering. The *Falcon* anchored off the coast, and passengers had to pay for native boatmen to shuttle them between the *Falcon* and the town of Chagres. Some of the crew jumped ship, for their chance in the gold fields. At one end of the bay, pronounced and regal, an old fort stood prominently upon a crested outcrop of limestone, abandoned and covered in jungle. The Spaniards built the fortress for protection from Caribbean pirates, who lay waiting for their plundered gold and silver. At this moment, Daniel began to realize that perhaps more thought for this adventure could have been pursued on his part. He was left with a simple lingering thought: *What was I thinking when I embarked on this wild journey?* Many of the men who boarded in New Orleans were so unsavory, Daniel and Philippe feared for their lives. The men had now entered a world with the wild breath of jungle, and sleeping under the canopy of trees awakened something in their past, where rivers met, brown and slurred. The isthmus was layered with lush jungle and sweltering heat. One could not discount the haunting memories of conquistadors, which loomed in the shadows. Their search for cities of gold had been lost and forgotten for centuries, while they peered into the canyons of their own reckless pursuit for wealth and the word of God. This history, locked into the landscape, loomed in Daniel's thoughts.

This leg of the journey began by canoe to the town of Cruces, forty-five miles upriver, with native porters, half-naked and their tongues wild, eager for the work but with a disdain for the foul-mannered Argonauts, drunken with lust for California gold. Fortunately for both Daniel and Philippe, traveling with the governor made this part of the journey less stressful, since he had planned the journey right down to the high tea. While the governor bartered for passage upriver, Philippe and Daniel sat near the docks.

Philippe said, "I feel so fortunate that the governor and his group have taken me in." Responding, Daniel said, "He is a kind and gentle man—that is, when you're on the same side of thought as he is." Suddenly there was a commotion about fifty yards down the beach. A woman began to scream in Spanish at a man no larger than her, and he screamed right back. Daniel and Philippe got up and walked toward them, and Daniel noticed a gull eating a sea star on the rocks while other gulls moved in for a taste. Getting closer, they saw the woman throw something at the man and then run away.

Daniel shouted, "Can we help?

Philippe interjected, "*Podemos ayudarle a usted, ¿está bien?* Can we help you, are you okay?"

Shaking his head and giving Philippe a shove, Daniel said, "And he speaks Spanish too?"

Philippe winked at Daniel and said, "What language does one with the last name of Galvez speak? Besides, my mother's attendant was Spanish."

As they neared they learned that the man was an oyster diver and caught the woman stealing his pearls, which were laid out neatly in arranged baskets woven of palm and ginger.

Daniel's eyes were wide and clear. "These are beautiful!" The pearls were arranged by size, from that of a small pea to a grape. With Philippe's help, he bartered the man from one hundred to twenty-six U.S. dollars. The diver took his machete and cut woven palm into a large square. He picked up the bowl and dropped the three grape-size pearls and sixty pea-size ones onto the palm sheet, which he quickly folded and tied into a freshly made envelope. As they turned, the governor was waving for them to hurry along.

Philippe questioned, "Why in tarnation do you want pearls?"

"My mother likes them."

In a teasing tone, Philippe poked, "You are a liar, Benet. These are for Claire McCarthy." He gave Daniel a playful shove.

Ignoring him, Daniel handed the pearls to his friend, and continued, "Lock these in that box of yours for me."

The Argonauts were left to barter for their passage, some paying as high as twenty dollars, which made their unsavory attitude even worse. The native canoes, called bungos, were carved from one tree and were about twenty-five feet in length. The governor's party of six bungos slowly snaked upriver. Monkeys jumped in the canopy as they responded to a cacophony of random gunshots by several drunken Argonauts playing target practice. The monkeys responded by throwing fruit upon their intruders, inviting more gunfire until the governor shouted, "Perhaps you might save your ammunition for those who may wish to do you wrong." Several men ignored the governor. Daniel and Philippe both kept to themselves, mostly wanting to live. At times, these men, with their lack of manners and decency, kept them on guard at all hours.

It wasn't long before it was clear that some men had some type of jungle sickness. Their faces were fatigued and flushed with fever.

By this point Daniel had developed a bonding friendship with Mr. Kent, twenty years his senior, who also held a disdain for the new members of the party. But Mr. Kent was now fevered, his body now limp and withdrawn.

As the travelers entered a village, they were greeted first by men seeking work, and then by half-naked children who ran in a pouring rain, odd for this time of year, laughing while slipping in the mud. There was a strange odor of rotted melons and urine on the hot breath of the jungle, and the village lay shuttered for siesta. The houses, huts really, were constructed of jungle wood and leaves with no windows. The men brought Mr. Kent, hot as fire, into the first hut and lay him out of the weather. His eyes were seas of glass, forlorn and without hope.

Daniel asked, "Are you comfortable?" Mr. Kent's face, vacant and shallow, pierced Daniel like a shattered dream. Mr. Kent did not respond.

The men sat with Mr. Kent into the evening, attempting to make him comfortable.

Finally, the next morning Mr. Kent said, "I am at the end of my trail on this great adventure. My new friends, this is where it ends, in a Godforsaken puddle of mud in the jungle, a fitting end for this old traveler."

Daniel said, "Let me get you some tea."

When he returned, Mr. Kent's trembling hands had grabbed Philippe's shirt and he said, "I have two requests: take this letter and my ticket from my bag and please deliver the letter to a Mr. Ashley Stewart. Use my ticket to board and you will meet him on the *SS California.*"

As Daniel wiped his fevered brow, Kent said, "Lads, can you find a big gold nugget for me and send a bit of it to my wife?"

Daniel sat and held him in death, wet with the rain, as his thoughts drifted backward, to the alleyway and Samuel Fairagain and then to his own father's death.

The next day the rain stopped, and by late afternoon the sun wavered lazily in the west. The party spent the morning and most of the afternoon attempting to dig a proper grave for Kent, with merely sticks and sharp rocks, produced a shallow, muddy resting place. As the rain began to once again drizzle, the governor, a man who had done this on the battlefield on many occasions, stepped forward and said, "I would like to say some verse that I feel is meaningful for the moment. The first is for our beloved Mr. Kent and his loving family, and the second is for all of us at this sad moment.

The righteous perish, and no one ponders it in his heart; devout men are taken away, and no one understands that the righteous are taken away to be spared from evil. Those who walk uprightly enter into peace; they find rest as they lie in death. Isaiah 57:1-2."

After a long moment of silence, the governor continued, *"For our light and momentary troubles are achieving for us an eternal glory that far outweighs them all. So we fix our eyes not on what is seen, but on what is unseen. For what is seen is temporary but what is unseen is eternal. 2Corinthians 4:17-18.*

"Anything else you would like to say, gentlemen?"

Moved by the governor's words, the men said their goodbyes and hoped and prayed that Kent might rest in peace.

******

Maeve asked, "Mom, do you think that the pearls are really for Daniel's mother, or are they for Claire?"

"Maeve, they were for Claire, you saw them in her ship captain's box," said Brodie.

"That seems a little farfetched, don't you think? Daniel has only seen her once, and it was certainly not a friendly encounter. He has no idea where she even is."

Maeve pondered on her mother's words, and said, "I think it's sweet that Daniel bought the pearls for his mother."

Brodie interjected, "And he put them in Philippe's pirate chest for safekeeping."

"Brodie," Maeve said, "Daniel and Philippe are not pirates, they're nice."

"Well, chickabiddies, if we keep reading we might find out the answer," pleaded Grammy.

"Mom, I would buy you pearls," Brodie cooed.

"What a nice thought, thank you my dear little B, that's very sweet," Vanessa said, giving her boy a loving squeeze. As Vanessa turned the page and began to read the next chapter, she noticed her Grammy looking at her with loving admiration. With that one look, Vanessa's body filled with an intimate warm feeling.

19

Home is a shelter from storms—all sorts of storms.

—William Benet

December 5, 1848

Dearest Uncle,

I awoke this morning to yet another horizon, vast and forever. The languid hues of immense ocean cast a vacillating rhythm against the imperial dawn, awakening to the east. The sameness of everything, day in and day out, has worn me into a state of loneliness. Yes, Ashley is with me, and without him this would be unfathomable. But he fills his days with the men playing games, and smoking and drinking, as I am left to sit with the five other ladies on board. They mainly speak of scripture and needlepoint and at times debate their bread-making strategies. I have found solace in writing in my diary and drawing, and enjoy playing my piano after dinner. I must say, though, I hope that once off this prison of a ship, I may never play "Oh, Susanna" again! The food is as tasteless as the behavior of the Argonauts. I am tired of fish and beans and the water is horrendous.

The tropical heat is stiflingly hot and the nights are unbearable. The men drench themselves with buckets of seawater, a practice I shall not take part in. We must stop in Valparaiso to resupply the ship. I long to eat fresh food, besides fish. The seas have been stormy and cold coming around the horn, and for some odd reason has given me some comfort, as if I am nearing Boston.
Loving thoughts,
Claire

20

—ALBERT F. SCHILIEDER

I joined the group out of boredom and also to prove Ashley wrong. Ashley had remarked to me that, "It's not needlepoint, it's meddle-point—women sitting around and meddling into everyone else's affairs."

I sat mesmerized by the ocean's swelling effect on the ship, on the deck with my five woman friends doing needlepoint.

As we sat, I said, "I finally confronted Ashley about his lack of attention to my needs. He knows how dreadfully I hate this cursed ship, the horrendous food, the infinite sea, the horizon that never ends, and how he carries his bravado around with the other gentleman and the drinking, my lord."

"Well, I might add, Claire," said Thelma, "try being married to a navy officer for sixteen years, and then we will talk."

Thelma's daughter, two years younger than I, continued, "Yes, all you do is move from place to place. Do you know how many places I have lived?"

Another woman, Frances, traveling with her sister Goldie, interjected quietly, "Perhaps Ashley just needs some motion on the ocean."

"What on Earth are you referring to?" I returned, my eyebrows now casting a V, faint but distinct.

"Just an old seaman expression," she answered. The sisters, perhaps in their late twenties, shyly smiled at each other.

I chewed on the thought as Goldie added, "Men are just who they are. I say, the good lord help them in the middle of winter with no one to chop the wood, cook their meals, and pick up after them. They just might shrivel up and evaporate."

Frances added, "Our mother used to say, 'Men are such simple things. The best way to get a man to do something you want is to suggest they are too old for it.'"

21

The cruelest thing a man can do to a woman is to portray her as perfection.

—D.H. Lawrence

The *California* reached Valparaiso on a calm morning, as cormorants lulled across the water. A beautiful bay greeted me in the shape of a cup, as steep Mediterranean mountains rose from the sea.

As I stepped off the ship holding Ashley's arm, I breathed deeply and said, "Amen, I am on solid ground and off that wretched ship." Within moments we were approached by three gentlemen who introduced themselves as directors of mail service in Valparaiso.

One gentleman, wearing broad fall-front trousers and a gray linen swallowtail coat, said, "Mr. Ashley Stewart, please come with us and allow us to show you our operation, our commitment and hospitality." Ashley looked at me, not knowing what to say or do.

Finally I asserted, flicking my wrist in the air, "Oh, you go ahead, I'll go investigate the shopping with the ladies." We hugged goodbye as I glanced at the ladies coming ashore, in particular two Chilean women clad in muslin dresses, with ebony hair and skin of a lightly roasted coffee bean, casting admiring glances at Ashley, who tipped his hat in their direction. I thought to myself, *Men, so despicable.*

The ladies were interested in shopping, but fresh food was first. The town was laid out nicely and quite a number of Yankees had made it their home for one reason or another. Everyone had his or her own story.

After a lovely lunch, we were approached by a gentleman whose walnut-colored skin and silky black hair shone in the in the afternoon light.

He said, *"Damas, buenas tardes, tu belleza irradia como el cielo. Mi nombre es Juan Méndez de Valparaíso."* "Ladies, good afternoon, your beauty radiates as the sky. My name is Juan Méndez of Valparaiso." He took my hand and kissed it, his warm eyes pierced with intent, and continued, *"Y tú mi dulce flor son?"* "And you are my sweet flower." My eyes now fixed upon the man's, I saw they were the color of gray mist. Suddenly the memory of the Paper White butterfly drifted like the smoke of a smoldering fire and rose to the surface of my thoughts, as my skin began to display a humid glaze from the moment.

Another gentleman interjected, "Please excuse my friend, ladies, he is merely introducing himself. He means no harm."

Goldie quipped, "Well, I would say, when a man introduces himself like that to a lady, it's trouble."

Frances retorted, "Well, he is a foreigner, and I thought it was gentlemanly."

I stepped back, flushed, as Ellen suggested they look for thread and yarn. I noticed a dress shop and with anticipation said to Goldie, "I will meet up with you at the mercantile. I want to look at the dresses."

Once inside, I slowly drew in my breath, and pondered again my encounter in the forest, the hues of celadon, Daniel Benet and the Paper White Butterfly. I felt embarrassed by the gentleman's brazenness, yet remained puzzled by my reoccurring attention to the encounter in the forest. I quickly distracted myself, thinking about what I might like to wear when I left the *California* for the last time.

22

Man spends his life in reasoning on the past,
in complaining of the present and fearing the future.

—Antoine Rivaol

January 20, 1849
Dearest Uncle,

Upon arrival, on December 17, in Callao, Peru, Ashley convinced Captain Forbes to take on one hundred gold seekers, which created quite the stir amongst the crew. He believed that the company could profit by taking advantage of the Gold Rush. The ship is now more crowded, and having so many men on board has made the women feel nervous, although Frances and Goldie appear to be enjoying the added interest.

In my opinion, it was incorrect of Ashley to add more passengers when the *California* is already contracted to pick up passengers in Panama City. The added passengers have crowded the living space and will stress the ship's supplies. This voyage seems to have changed Ashley greatly. He is no longer the doting new husband, and he has enjoyed the popularity of the other men, as the ship's agent. He now appears to be swimming in his own vanity. I have expressed my concerns, yet they have gone unnoticed. I went shopping in both Valparaiso and Callao and purchased some new clothes, as I refuse to wash my garments in saltwater, and the fresh water, Ashley says, is only for drinking and preparing food.

Oh, Uncle, how I miss Watuppa Pond and your calm and loving presence in my life, and Levi too. I miss riding Bluebell in the woods and having Sweet Pea snuggle my feet as I read on the porch. How I wish for this journey to end. It is my hope that we will get off this prison of a ship at Panama City and return to you and Watuppa Pond. I guess you could say I have been stricken hard with a real New England spring fever.

With love,
Claire

23

*In a world where death is the hunter, my friend there
is no time for regrets or doubts. There is only time for decisions.*

—Carlos Castaneda

After two weeks, Philippe had the woman limping around their makeshift camp and she was healing. He gave her a sewing kit to repair her clothes and her first words to him were, *"Pourquoi voudriez-vous m'aider, quel est-il que vous voulez?"* "Why would you help me, what is it you want?" She spoke perfect French with a refined elegance and dignity.

Philippe responded, *"Nous devons tous continuer à nous battre pour ce qui est droit."* "We all must continue to fight for what is right."

"You could have been killed, and why for someone unknown to you?" she continued in perfect English. He learned that her name was Gracie Métoyer and that she was from Yucca Plantation, in Natchitoches Parish. Her family, of French and African origin, had been living on the land for six generations, and she had escaped an arranged marriage by her father to a drunken associate. No dowry would ever be large enough for such an arrangement. So she set off for Baton Rouge and possibly New Orleans.

"I had grand plans until those two bounty hunters found me."

"I will help get you there the best I can. Do you know anyone or have a place to go in Baton Rouge?"

Gazing as the smoke rose through the frozen morning chill, she said, "Only my father's friends. One has a daughter my age, she is the only one."

With that, Philippe got up from the small fire, handed her his baby dragoon, grabbed his rifle, and said, "I'm going to see if I can get us something to eat." He walked out of the glen and into the woods. The briars were thick and full of life and grouse exploded to life as he came near. At 25 yards, Philippe saw a hare, with its long pointed ears reaching skyward, frozen with purposeful intent. Philippe slowly raised his rifle in the silence as Gracie's scream from the distance shattered the moment and the hare scampered away in a flash. Philippe leapt through the briars toward the camp.

Once again, a bounty hunter had Gracie frantically struggling to free herself. Her new captor was a huge hulk of a man, about six feet five inches. Philippe tracked on the barrel of his rifle and yelled, "Let her go or you're a dead man!"

The man brought his knife to Gracie's throat as she continued to struggle in his vise-like grip, and said, "Drop that there weapon of yours, mister, or I slit her throat."

"I don't bluff, my friend, especially when it comes to my property. Gracie is no runaway," barked Philippe.

Without further thought, Philippe squeezed the trigger and the rifle blast fractured the silence, hitting the man just below his throat as he was thrown backward, still holding Gracie, as she fell with him onto his stomach. Blood erupted from her mouth and Philippe realized the man had a second knife at her back, and she had fallen onto the knife. He quickly rolled her off of him, to help her breathe, and removed the knife, trying to stop her bleeding.

"Thank you for the second chance, Philippe," she managed in a raspy voice, her eyelids fading.

"Don't talk, focus on your breathing."

Slowly Philippe saw her color evaporate and her breathing stopped. She was gone.

Suddenly, an upwelling of fear overtook him. "I have killed three men and now Gracie," he said aloud, as if someone was listening. He pulled the man as best he could into the briars, attempted a shallow grave for Gracie, and left for the river, the quickest way to New Orleans and his mother.

Philippe's mother, Katherine, lived in a converted blacksmith shop of his father's at 941 Bourbon Street, New Orleans, where she rented several rooms with the help of Carmelita, her longtime attendant, who had helped raise Philippe. He hoped his mother could help him get on a boat to somewhere, as it was not in his plans to be hung for murder. Upon his arrival in New Orleans, word of gold being discovered in California was spreading like a wildfire of hope. Philippe's mother had connections and somehow, only one day after arriving in New Orleans, his ticket to California appeared.

She also handed him some money in a patch of deer hide and said, "This was your father's, and he left it for the both of us for safe keeping. Since hearing of his passing, I wanted you to have it. All I know is that it is a map to somewhere, more than likely in the Caribbean. Knowing your father, it must be something valuable."

****

"Mom, I think Philippe is the hero," Maeve said. "He is so brave and fearless. He really cares about what's right," She then handed her mother the manuscript.

Brodie added, "Philippe is awesome! Anybody who messes with him is dead."

"Well, little B, sometimes in doing the right thing, bad things happen," said Grammy. Vanessa pondered the weight of the words as she watched her Grammy smile at her babies, and drew a relaxed and hopeful breath as she began to read.

24

Coincidences link us to the unknown and weave us into it.

—Doug Dillon

The journey by canoe ended at the edge of the jungle, with Mr. Kent's passing. From there the governors' party then proceeded on mules over rugged mesas and across savannahs of scorched jungle converted to growths of wild bananas, papaya, and pineapple, the landscape sparsely speckled with pigs and chickens. The lurking smell of burnt jungle loomed. The natives carved out their lives, and as feeble as it might seem, they were joyous and content. Once on a mule, both Daniel and Philippe felt that they had returned to an element over which they had some control. Daniel's mind was filled with thoughts of his dear friend Buttons, whose fate he now pondered. Five days after leaving the *Falcon,* the adventurous party paused and looked down for the first time upon the Pacific Ocean and the seaport of Panama. They had traveled more than fourteen miles by land and twenty-six miles in a bungo and were fatigued and worn from the journey. They stared out at the blue waters of the Pacific Ocean, which seemed a vacant impossibility just a year ago and was now before them.

The Governor's party was naively eager to board the *California* and continue the journey to California after ten days in the jungle, with the stifling heat, bad water, sickness, and Mr. Kent's death. To their dismay, when they reached the port, hundreds of men were waiting to board the *California,* which had not yet arrived. While the governor's party waited for its arrival, they shifted back into their daily routine on the *Falcon,* rotating from dominoes to poker than back to dominoes, while eating fish with flavors new and bold.

On the fifth day, the *California* arrived in Panama. As the steamer entered the bay, a rash of gunfire erupted on shore, to the startled amazement of all those on board. The ship was carrying one hundred Peruvian gold seekers, who had boarded in Lima, and as news of the Peruvians on board circulated among the crowd, a riotous mood spread through the awaiting Argonauts. Men began shooting their pistols and chartering boats to take them to the waiting ship, so that they could board and push the foreigners off.

The ship anchored off shore, to allow the loading of coal and supplies. Daniel was impressed by the governor's character, along with his calm demeanor, as he attempted to reach a compromise in the dispute. But it was Captain Cleveland Forbes who initiated the truce. The Peruvians would stay and the next three days would be spent building proper accommodations for all on board, as well as stockpiling food and fuel, as the increased weight of the ship increased fuel requirements. The staterooms were converted to sleep many, and hammocks and makeshift sleeping quarters were built on the deck.

******

As Ashley gazed to the shore, the only words from his mouth were, "Oh, my God, what have I created?"

As I took his arm I said, "What is all of the commotion, Ashley, dear?"

"Well, from the looks of it there are over five hundred men wanting to board."

I replied, "I told you it was a mistake taking on the Peruvians."

"Claire, when we left New York, we had only sold passage for thirty-five! How could I have predicted this rush for gold and the fever it has created?"

"My dear Ashley, it appears that you have dollars clouding your eyes."

"Claire, when we get to San Francisco you will have the best of what those dollars can buy," Ashley replied.

My skin now flushed and tight, I pouted, "Money can't buy what I want."

Sidestepping a bit and holding my gaze, he said, "What are you saying?"

"Oh, Ashley, I so wish for your companionship. We have been on this boat for months. I am lonely, Ashley, and you spend most of your time with those men."

"Claire, as you know, I am the agent for this ship and with that comes responsibilities."

My eyes shooting a piercing turquoise, I said, "Right, like gambling, smoking, and drinking."

I grabbed my book and stepped firmly out of the stateroom and onto the deck as a curtain of orange was melting into an azure sea, with a backdrop of surging green forests. I walked to the bow, sat facing the horizon, as a silent anger boiled inside of me. The rhythmic swells of the sea slowly rocked and soothed me, as I gazed into the jungle and its lovely shade of green peas, rising from the sea with a melting sky. My thoughts floated off, to the memory of my Delaine dress and those eyes of Daniel Benet. I pondered why I had hastily married Ashley and allowed myself to be held prisoner on this ship for months. How I longed for Watuppa Pond, my uncle, Levi, Bluebell, and my dog, Sweet Pea. That evening, I did not play the piano and left for my cabin directly after dinner.

25

There was quite a commotion on the docks as boarding started
the next day, with guns firing in the air and people bullying
others for their tickets. The Governor's party was the first to board
the *California,* giving Daniel and Philippe a welcomed relief from
the raucous crowd of Argonauts.

After the morning meal, I took my book to the bow and sat reading as the morning sky opened up on the bay, mirrored upon rolling
swells. It was hard for me to read as I continued to chew upon the
events of the night before.

I looked up from my book and noticed a boat approaching the
steamer, and said aloud with disdain, "My God, it is already beginning." With that, I retreated to my chair in the stateroom while
Ashley finished dressing.

The shout of a man roared into the cabin, "Persifor Smith party,
Military Governor of California requesting to board."

"Good morning, my dear Claire," cooed Ashley.

"Oh, is it?" I sarcastically retorted.

"Did you sleep well?"

"Actually, no, under the circumstances. I have spent the night pondering our decisions in this charade. The drunkards are already starting to board." My voice resonated across the steamer. I slumped in the chair with obvious disdain.

Ashley, in a sugary voice, attempted to soothe his despondent bride. "I will solve this mess," he said as a knock on the door suddenly startled us both. "Yes, who is it?" Ashley asked.

"Mr. Stewart, the Persifor Smith party has boarded and the governor wishes to speak with you," the man said.

As Ashley stepped onto the deck, the morning was already stiflingly humid. He approached the party. I stayed slouched in the chair as introductions were made on deck.

"Welcome aboard," I heard Ashley greet the party.

"Good morning, sir, I am General Persifor Smith, let me introduce to you to my beautiful wife, Ellen. This is Mr. Philippe Galvez, and he has been asked to deliver a letter to you."

"It's nice to meet you, Mr. Stewart. Our friend Mr. Kent, before he passed on, asked me to deliver this to you," Philippe said as he handed Ashley the letter.

The Governor continued the introductions. Finally he said, "And lastly, we have this interesting young man, Mr. Daniel Benet."

I was suddenly alert. "It cannot be him," I stammered to myself. A wildfire of sensation scampered along my backbone.

Daniel stepped toward Ashley and held out his hand in greeting, saying, "Benet, Daniel Benet," and shaking his hand.

Now a slow tingle crept under my skin. "Why, it cannot be him!" I repeated to myself, as I left the chair and entered the open doorway.

Daniel's eyes wandered over Ashley's shoulder toward the stateroom door, to where I stood. My face was saturated in confusion, yet focused. My eyes radiated back at him, full of aquamarine, watching his own obvious disbelief rapidly spreading across his face.

Nervous perspiration pooled on my upper lip, as I stared back at him. Ashley noticed the angle of Daniel's gaze and turned to see me at the stateroom door. "Claire, let me introduce you to our guests." I sauntered to Ashley's side. "Claire, this is General Persifor Smith and his wife, Ellen, Mr. Philippe Galvez, and Mr. Daniel Benet."

Ashley met my gaze, then turned to the group and gestured, "And my lovely wife, Claire."

"Nice to meet all of you, welcome aboard the *California*," I responded with cultured precision. My entire body shuddered, as if I were falling into an endless sinkhole.

******

My lord, Daniel thought to himself, *what's happening here? How is this now all going to unfold?*

Daniel was told upon boarding that he and Philippe would share a stateroom with eight men, and the new room was in the ship's library, which had been transformed into sleeping quarters. Before the other inhabitants boarded, he found a book, *Les Trois Mousquetaires*, *The Three Musketeers* by Alexander Dumas.

"Have you heard of this book?" he asked Philippe.

"Ah! Dumas! *Les Trois Mousquetaires!* His style of the written word will transport you away from this circumstance and ship to a place wild and timeless."

Yes, the ship, Daniel pondered, *which I asked for, has duly sequestered my life.* But he was too far into the adventure to complain.

Philippe and Daniel chose the best corner near the door, to avoid feeling trapped. Together they began to assess how to secure their belongings. Lucky for Daniel, Philippe came prepared, as he had brought a locked box for security.

Suddenly Daniel was flooded back with the memory of his very own words echoing throughout the forest, as mud flew off his cheek and onto a backdrop of green. The thought lingered as a salmon does at the base of a waterfall, before its leap.

"Where did you just float off to?" Philippe asked him.

He blushed. "The woman in the woods, the one I told you about."

"Yes, what about her?"

"It is her, she is here on this ship! Now what do I do?"

"What are you talking about?"

"Ashley's wife! It is her, Philippe. Claire," he said with hushed breath, his face anguished and full of desperation.

Philippe's eyes scanned Daniel's, which shimmered with something lost, and he said, *"Mon Dieu, Benet! Vous êtes voué et pas heureux!"*

"Excuse me?" he said, waiting for a translation.

"My God, Benet! You are doomed and not happy!" Philippe continued to probe, "How can this be so, that she is here, on this ship?"

"A bloody twist of fate, I suppose. Now what do I do? I have no bloody idea how women operate."

"You need to talk to her."

"And just how will I do that, Philippe?"

"Go to the bow with your sketch pad and draw. She will approach you, trust me."

Images of their meeting flooded Daniel with the color of celadon, cascading before him.

"Benet! *Écoutez-vous?* Are you listening?"

Coming back to the moment, as the green sea filled his vision he said, "Yes, and what is it exactly you propose that I say to her when she approaches?"

"You will tell her the truth. She is a married woman. Why would you be a threat to her or her husband? You know neither her nor him."

"Philippe, this is nonsense, she will not approach me."

26

February 12, 1849

Dear Uncle,

We're moving slowly in this endless landscape of ocean. The storms come on swiftly and vanish at the same pace. We experienced a very severe gale from the northwest, which began in the morning and kept increasing until after midnight, and it blew very heavy, with tremendous swells churning the sea.

Ashley received a letter in Panama, which bore bad news. The gentleman who was overseeing our living arrangements and securing a building for the U.S Mail Steamship Company apparently passed away. I'm quite worried about our fate once we reach San Francisco.

As we docked in Acapulco for supplies, a stowaway was discovered. Also exposed was a fireman on board, who snuck the man onto the ship. They were both ordered in shackles, yet the crew threatened mutiny and chaos ensued. Captain Forbes gave the crew two days' rest to cool off. Walking beyond the ship has been a long-awaited respite. I had all of my clothes laundered and a real bath. Ashley is still under the weather and is as stubborn as ever, and his cough rattles more each day. He leaves me for long periods during the day to attend to business, play games with the men, and to drink and smoke. I try to tell him he needs rest, but he refuses. It is like his whole purpose in life is the Pacific Mail Steamship Company. My growing disdain for Ashley sits tempered on my shoulder because Ashley is never there for me. I fear that my marriage to Ashley was a hasty schoolgirl mistake.

I spend my days writing in my journal or reading, as I am bored with sketching. There have been times when I dreaded playing the piano in the evening, playing the same songs over and over. I miss you, Uncle, and Watuppa Pond too! There are days when I lay dreaming of bolting from the barn with Bluebell with the wind dancing upon my face, flushed with the cool of morning, only to wake to the same sea, endless and alone. The crowding is unbearable to say the least. The men who boarded from Panama are a ruthless lot, fevered with gold and whiskey. Their catcalls to the women are insulting and I thank the few men who step up to stop it. Being imprisoned on this ship with these vile wretched creatures will stain my memory forever.

With love,

Claire

27

Let men tremble to win the hand of women, unless they win along with it the utmost passion of her heart.

—Nathaniel Hawthorne

"So tell me, what do you think of Mr. Stewart?" asked Philippe.

"Well, not as highly as his bride. He seems full of himself and his position."

"Yes, it is clear as to who is in his camp."

"And that means?"

"It means you better watch yourself around him and his wife."

"We have not spoken a word to each other. I will not deny that she is somewhat of a distraction to me."

"Somewhat of a distraction to both of you!" Stepping closer to Daniel, Philippe whispered with clenched teeth, his intent clear, "You get this girl out your head. Do you hear me? Are you listening? She will get you killed and thrown into this bloody sea."

"Philippe, what have I done for anyone to think anything?"

"See the governor over there?"

"Yes."

Philippe's face began to gape at the governor with the innocent eyes of a puppy.

"I do not do that!"

"You think you are not? People are beginning to notice, my friend."

"We will see. Good night."

"Good night."

28

Not everything that is faced can be changed
but nothing can be changed until it's faced.

—JAMES BALDWIN

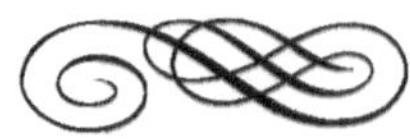

At dawn Daniel awoke to dripping water from the deck above caused by a storm in the night. He grabbed Dumas and his sketchbook and set out for the stern as the steam from the rain hovered in the morning light.

He gazed at the flight of the sea birds across the horizon, scattered like lost words, hungry and tormented. He thought, *No more birds,* and flipped through his sketches, stopping at an unfinished scene from Chagres and the bungos. His thoughts drifted back to Mr. Kent and his promise to Kent's wife and family, to bring back a nugget for them. He began to work on the sketch, and the dampness rested upon the charcoal, cementing it to the page. Suddenly he heard footsteps behind him, and turned and saw Claire approaching.

"I must have words with you," I announced to Daniel on the deck of the ship.

He caught my eyes, dancing in the morning light.

"Good morning, my lovely friend," he said, his eyes piercing the space between us. "Isn't the light exquisite right now?"

Daniel suddenly felt a sharp pain on his cheek.

"How dare you speak to me in such a manner, Mr. Benet. I am a married woman and I will not tolerate such vileness."

"Ma'am, I mean no disrespect."

"Is that all you have to say, Mr. Benet?"

"My name is Daniel."

"Daniel, you make me nervous, to the point of screaming! You must stop gawking at me—the crew, the passengers are all suspicious."

"And you know this because?"

"I don't, but please refrain until we get off this godforsaken ship."

Daniel's face now danced playfully. "So what will happen when we arrive in San Francisco?"

"I do not know. Good day, Daniel."

I felt Daniel's gaze follow me as I headed starboard. Glancing back I saw him catching himself, as he returned to his sketchpad.

****

"Claire is defending her honor," Maeve said. "Right, Mommy?"

"Yes, honey, she wants everyone to know that she is a respectable woman who does the right thing."

"I think she has the hots for Daniel," said Brodie.

"Brodie, Claire is married!" Maeve said. "She does not want to be with anyone else, she's married to Ashley."

"Excuse me, Brodie, 'the hots'? Just where do you pick this language up?" his mother inquired.

"I think that Daniel and Philippe will kill Ashley in a sword fight."

Vanessa interjected, "Come on, you two, stop it, no one is going to kill anyone," glancing at her Grammy as if to say, *Right?*

Grammy said, "Chickabiddies, it is not the path we take, it's the end result that's important. You both need to think about the end result."

Brodie said, "The end result of what, Grammy?"

Leaning toward him, her face wrinkled and pinched, Grammy said, "Oh, child! The pouting, the loathing, the empathy for the human struggle of life, it is all part of it. I most certainly have had many paths in my life, many of which I did not choose. But little man, they all led to this here mohair couch."

"Why didn't you choose your paths, Grammy?"

"Brodie, sometimes life gives you a roadblock or two."

"Like a roundabout, Grammy?" Maeve asked.

"That's it, chickabiddy, a roundabout."

"What kind of roadblocks did you have, Grammy?" Brodie questioned.

"One was the day I found your great-grandfather dead in the garden. He had been picking a cabbage. Then there was the day I lost my twins, William and Margret, their spouses, and my granddaughter Emily." Her voice cracked as she continued, "Those roadblocks changed me into another person— a person I am not particularly fond of." She wagered a forlorn glance in Vanessa's direction then repeated, "We all have our own roadblocks in life. It is just part of the story, little man. Let's listen."

Suddenly Vanessa felt the sky opening in her dark cloud of emotions.

29

Truth, like light, blinds. Falsehood, on the contrary,
is a beautiful twilight that encounters every object.

—ALBERT CAMUS

After two weeks, the coal for the engines was gone and a riotous dark cloud permeated the ship. During the evening meal, arguments erupted about what Captain Forbes should or should not do.

One portly man shouted into the crowd, "We need to use all available wood to fuel the steamer and reach San Francisco." The captain had urged all passengers to collect wood on the coastal islands five days away.

"But you said that we had wood for one day."

Yet another man shouted, "And there is no wind."

"We can take apart the sleeping hassocks and burn the lumber," said another.

"Yes, we can sleep on the decks!" one man shouted.

"Just get us to San Francisco!" yelled another.

The motley crowd was a boiling pot. As in Panama, Ashley, the Captain, and the governor caucused and the resulting decision was almost the undoing of the voyage. They would collect the wood used to build bunks in Panama to fuel the ship the rest of the way to San Francisco. Once the decision was announced, a frenzied riot erupted among the male passengers, who began tearing apart whatever they could. Everyone was on deck, many just spectators. My group of women had been sitting with our needlepoint and now watched the pillage, aghast. Daniel and Philippe were standing on top of the main cabin, urging the men to calm down.

One man yelled, "Let's get rid of that damn piano!"

"Yes, we don't need that!" shouted another man.

"You will not touch that piano!" shouted Daniel.

Now stomping my way into the altercation, I screamed, "You will not touch my piano, you nasty vermin!"

As the riotous men moved toward the galley, Daniel leapt from the top of the cabin and Philippe followed. Frozen in disbelief, I watched a man pick up a spar from the rigging and say to Daniel, "Out of my way, boy."

As he lifted the spar to smash the piano, Daniel landed a hard punch to the man's jaw, knocking him backward onto the deck. Immediately he was mauled, and Philippe joined in to protect his friend.

A loud scream, from the deepest depths of my body, flew across the water, like a dying horse. "Noooo!" The crashing ring of my dying piano echoed, its last piece, refracting a muzzled tone of Tchaikovsky's "Pathétique Symphony" in forte, its gloried and adventurous story in one last violent crescendo. The sudden crack of the governor's dragoon brought silence to the rampage. Unfortunately, however, the damage had been done. There was a mulled silence. My piano was ruined. My face flooding in tears, my nostrils flared, I glared nastily at the men and yelled, "You are barbaric animals and I hope you all burn in hell!"

A crowd of men descended on the piano like a pack of frenzied wolves, breaking it to pieces. I glanced silently at Ashley with a scathing scorn, as if to say, *you miserable coward! You stood there and did nothing!*

At this point the ship was split: those who cared about the piano and those who did not. I retreated to my cabin with Ashley in tow. My piano was gone, my only friend, shattered and consumed by fire in minutes. I lay there mute, even through Ashley's consoling. I just turned off my life, a closed sign drawn upon my face, a silent army brewing inside my heart.

The next day, under clear skies and a whispering wind, one hundred sacks of coal were discovered in the hold behind a load of lumber. When told, I slipped further down the slope of my anguish.

30

Resentment is like taking poison and
waiting for the other person to die.

—Malachy McCourt

February 26, 1849

Dearest Uncle,

Shortly after leaving Mazatlán, the ship ran out of coal and the captain allowed the men to strip the hammocks. A near riot ensued, and in its fury my piano was destroyed and burned in minutes. Two men attempted to stop the destruction, and a fight ensued, but they were unsuccessful. All the while Ashley stood silent. I have since fallen into a deep sadness and sequestered myself in the cabin. I am so angered at Ashley, for not defending my honor or my piano. The entire ordeal was humiliating. I feel as though I cannot forgive him.

Today, we had a breath of fresh air, and hope, as the *California* came into Monterey Bay, a wide sweeping wheel of white sand and big trees painted

like a tapestry against the backdrop of vibrant greens shrouded in a foggy wetness. The bay was calm, laden with forests of kelp and sea otters, which dive swiftly for crabs and crack them with a rock while floating on their backs. Why, it is just the cutest thing. The best part of Monterey Bay has been that many of the men who boarded in Panama disembarked for the gold fields. Many had formed companies to work together, mainly for protection. Ashley remains ill and committed as ever to this company. I feel, as though, I will never forgive him for not being the man I thought he was when I married him. We shall arrive in San Francisco in three days and this dreadful adventure of my husband's will be behind me.
With love,
Claire

****

Maeve interjected, "I think Claire doesn't love Ashley anymore and they are going to get divorced."

"Hold on there my sweet chickabiddy," Grammy cooed. "They just got married, and besides couples didn't divorce then like they do now. They toughed it out and made a life of it."

"I think Ashley and Daniel will sword fight just like pirates. If Daniel loses, Philippe will kill Ashley," said Brodie.

"It's just a story, children, just listen," Vanessa pleaded with pursed lips.

Maeve said, "It's not just a story, Mom."

"I know, Maeve, it's our story." Suddenly her life and Claire's life appeared quite similar.

"When's the sword fight, Grammy?" Brodie asked.

"Perhaps soon, let's find out, little man."

Vanessa's thoughts drifted away as Maeve began to read.

31

Knocking on Heaven's door...

—BOB DYLAN

The *California* entered San Francisco Bay, eighty-eight days after leaving New York. A frenzied excitement bloomed across the ship. Guns fired and shots of whiskey were consumed as everyone reveled in the moment. The sisters held hands with big round eyes, flooded with anticipation and excitement as they contemplated the moments ahead. The married women rejoiced at the hope of finally returning to a family routine, by now long forgotten.

Ashley had been working for hours in preparation for going ashore. All of our belongings had been packed; the last thing he needed to do was unscrew the ship captain's box from its hold on the ship. I had pouted at its purchase, feeling it wasn't suited for a dignified lady. He attempted to assure me that very rough seas lay ahead and the box was well made and designed so it could be secured to the deck by screws.

"It's so big, I could never journal or write letters, let alone draw," I moped. But after the first storm, I had heard other passengers complaining about how their things had been tossed about in their cabins, and I admired Ashley's forethought. *What a clever contraption,* I had thought, *and these hidden compartments are adorable, quite clever actually, just like my husband.*

Ashley began once again to feel nauseous and somewhat faint. Fevered and perspiring, he began to unscrew the box from its traveling home. I sat on the deck with the women doing needlepoint. Thrills of anticipation, after months at sea, percolated the mood of the ship.

Breaking the silence, Frances said, "I wonder what will become of Mr. Benet and Mr. Galvez?"

Thelma said, in a knowing tone, "Well, what do you think?"

Goldie interjected, "I sure am going to miss looking at them."

Thelma now listed forward, and her skin thin and taut, she said, "Young lady, that is not how a proper lady talks."

"I'm just being honest."

Frances joined in, her eyes full and bright, and said, "Well, Thelma, one must admit that they both are pleasing to look at."

I sat in my new dress, mohair and mauve, bought for this very occasion in Valparaiso, quietly working my needlepoint, pretending not to be listening but thinking that I too would miss looking at them.

As a parting gesture, the men allowed the women to exit first, along with the governor's party, but Captain Forbes gave the women a stern warning. "I hate to say this, ladies, but you are about to enter a lawless city of mostly men. I urge that, for your safety, you do not make eye contact, or converse with anyone."

With faces now narrowed, Goldie and Frances grabbed hold of each other's hand. Ashley had insisted that I go ahead with the first group so he could bring closure to the voyage. There was his precious cargo, the mail, which could take weeks to organize and deliver, along with finding a new crew. For weeks, Ashley had lobbied the crew with certain favors if they would refrain from jumping ship for the gold fields, and he was determined to be the last man off the boat.

In a fatherly gesture, the governor offered his men to safely escort myself and the other women to the hotel. My face flushed at the news, but I disguised my embarrassment, as my anticipation began to brew. At the other end of the ship, after hearing of their assignment to deliver Claire and the other ladies to their hotel, Philippe leaned close to his friend, glared, and said, "Damn, Shanghaied twice. Don't you even look at her Daniel, if you get me killed, Benet, I will never forgive you!"

"What are you...?" Daniel said, smiling at him.

"I am warning you, Benet, not even a glance, or I will seriously knock you out."

Behind them, a backdrop of deserted boats, their masts sloping upon swells of hope, danced against the stark, hilly landscape. Tents crawled up the hill in military lines, as broad rows of fabric undulated in the soft breeze. Daniel's thoughts wandered as he peeled back the layers of their friendship, from almost two months of travel.

He turned to his friend, tipped his hat, and said with a wink, "I appreciate you looking out for me, Philippe. You are my friend, and my new business partner."

Once the boats were loaded, Daniel stepped to the stern, drinking in the land of tents and mud. He did not turn around as Philippe flirted with the sisters while he assisted them in boarding the skiff.

One by one, I watched my belongings go from one boat to the next. As my ship captain's box left the deck of the *California*, I remembered how ornery I had been and how I now loved my writing box. Just then, the man carrying the box tripped on some rope and the box fell into the bay, bobbing in the afternoon tide.

I turned to Goldie and said, "Well, Ashley did say it was waterproof and that it would float...so it appears Ashley was right."

The women stood there, watching the rescue as the box bobbed on the outgoing tide. Two stevedores rowed out and caught up with the box. The men struggled with it, as the box was bulky, and when they finally wrestled it onboard the weight of the box nearly sank the small craft, tilting it to one side. The ladies gave a short round of applause for the rescue effort.

After stepping onto the skiff, my skin was freshened by my first California breeze. I couldn't believe that it was the dead of winter, because it felt warmer than 50 degrees. Thoughts of my uncle and the New England winter reminded me of my loneliness. My gaze folded into the rolling landscape of tents, hoping my accommodations would be more suitable than on the *California*. As the boat neared the dock, catcalls rolled off the injudicious tongues of souls lost in a surge of anarchy, and traveled over the ripples of late afternoon water, toward the boat full of women and five men. Sailors ran around busily with ropes and hand spokes to keep the vessel from the neighboring boats, until finally the skiff reached the place where a plank could be shoved from the wharf, for a narrow footbridge.

32

Just when I think I learned the way to live, life changes.

—HUGH PRATHER

The Governor pulled out his dragoon and fired, as the sky was breaking fresh and clear with a bustling wind. With the pistol's crack, he turned to the men on the dock and said, "Gentlemen, I am Persifor Smith, the new Military Governor of the California territory, and I expect you to treat my party with the dignity and respect they deserve, or you will meet the barrel of my dragoon. Do we understand each other, gentlemen?"

Philippe and Daniel couldn't wait to take their first step onto California soil. For months they had thought about this moment, finally stepping off the boat. They had grown to hate the ship, and Daniel, I am sure, was looking forward to finally ridding himself of me, who still obsessed his thoughts. He wondered where he and Philippe would go, where they would sleep.

As the stevedores grabbed the ropes for docking, Philippe jumped to the dock, happy to be in San Francisco. He winked at his friend, than held his hand out to me, warmly looked into my eyes, and said, "Welcome to San Francisco, Mrs. Claire."

I took his hand for support crossing the plank, and with a warm and luscious smile, said, "Thank you, Mr. Galvez," with a cultured curtsy.

Daniel was the last man off the skiff, and Philippe gave him a big hug and said, "Welcome to California, my friend and business partner. Let's go find some nuggets."

"Which way to get a room for the night?" Daniel asked one of the stevedores. The man, his face chiseled, blank, and vacant, gestured with his head, his cigar-smoke wafting in the afternoon breeze toward the city of tents, marching up the hill.

"Hurry, Philippe, let's go."

"What is your hurry, my friend? We are free!"

"I want to know where Persifor is taking her."

"My God, Benet, when will this end? She is married."

As planned, Ashley was the last man before the captain to leave the *California,* after three months at sea. I am sure he hoped to heal the wounds of his behavior with me, and wondered what their new home looked like, as it was to be purchased during the trip. He was now sweating profusely, with chills surging through his body. He was experiencing periods of dizziness, which left him confused, for moments at a time. As he approached the gangplank, he became faint and dizzy, his forehead lathered in perspiration. His legs buckled and he suddenly fell, hitting his head on the edge of the ship, plunging wildly with a belly flop into the bay. Members of the crew jumped into the bitter cold water after him, and dragged his lifeless frame onto the wharf with considerable effort. With all of the commotion, Daniel and Philippe ran back to the dock to see what had happened. One stevedore emptied a bucket of water on Ashley, to revive him to consciousness. Another slapped his face, telling him to wake up. Ashley's face, bloodied and visibly swollen, was vacant and listless. A tall man in a red flannel shirt and jackboots checked for a pulse.

"He is already gone, gentlemen. Does anyone know him?"

Daniel, in shock, answered, "Well, he was in charge of the mail shipments. He is Ashley Stewart. His wife just left with the governor's party."

******

A hush of breath spread out over the room as Grammy's cat, Murphy, lay purring in the windowsill.

Maeve, her face contorted with drooping cheeks, cried out, "He dies! Ashley dies? Ashley can't just die!"

Brodie added, his face sullen, "I guess there's no sword fight. I wanted them to sword fight."

Vanessa said, in a melancholy tone, "It's all so very sad."

Her memory spilled like fresh paint onto the floor, dripping through the floorboards of her thoughts. Her parents' death, the months, the years, of the heart wrenching pain, and so much death in Claire's life too. It was as if Claire's life was reflecting back to her own.

Grammy, noticing her granddaughter deep in thought, gave a loving sigh and leaned in toward Brodie, her eyes blue and wide like marbles, and said, "And the plot thickens."

*Life is like a coin. You can spend it any way you wish,
but you can only spend it once.*

—Lillian Dickson

Daniel and Philippe attempted to follow the governor's party though streets of mud and frenzied activity. It was a swarming hive with thousands of bees. Tents and crudely made shacks lined the streets and as the governor's party turned up Market Street a gentle rain began to fall. Their wagon now stopped at a large wooden hotel on a busy corner.

With an exasperated sigh, Philippe stared blankly at his friend and said, "Are you now satisfied, Mr. Benet?"

Daniel approached a man who appeared to have not bathed in months and said, "Excuse me, sir, could you kindly direct us to where we may obtain room and board for the night?"

The man, his breath liquored and obviously intoxicated, turned to face them, finally regaining his balance, pointed into the crowd and said, "Go through the saloon there, and you will come out the other side."

Daniel and Philippe looked at each other, shrugged their shoulders, and stepped out over the mud and onto the boardwalk. They entered a large room with a drunken haze of men and several loosely dressed women. Once through the saloon, which was also a gambling hall and boarding house, they stepped out onto a street of wooden buildings, and saw several tents and lean-tos up a short hill.

Philippe bent down and began to stuff his trousers into his boots, and Daniel followed his lead. Both stepped off the boardwalk onto a bed of mud and sunk ankle-deep, then headed tenaciously up the hill. They heard music coming from a building that said *Exchange Office* over the door. Intrigued, they entered to find more drinking, more gambling and gold, all under a hovering cloud of cigar smoke.

A young Chilean woman approached them and said, "Fresh off the ocean, I see," while winking at Philippe. "Are you ready to blow off some steam?" The woman was radiant, with her white muslin dress against sepia skin and ebony hair. Philippe and Daniel caught each other staring at her, as she led them to a table along the periphery of the room. She snapped her fingers at the bartender as she looped her arm into Philippe's. Before Philippe and Daniel could sit down, a bottle of whiskey and three glasses arrived.

The woman began, "I am Maria and I believe that we're here for the same things."

Philippe's blue eyes crashed into her as he said, "And what might that be, Maria?"

Her brown eyes curved back into him as she moved closer and said, "For wealth." She poured three shots of whiskey.

Daniel sat silent as he watched the brown liquid flow into the glass. Another woman snuggled against him and said, "Hey sailor."

He threw back his whiskey and said, "Philippe, I will be right back," and headed for the door.

"Hey, Daniel, wait, where are you going?" But he was out the door and gone.

Maria snapped, "You stupid wench, you scared him off!"

No matter," the other woman said as she slid into Philippe's other arm. "I do not mind sharing him with you." She poured herself a whiskey.

As Daniel's boots hit the mud, his mind flashed back to the Delaine dress, and Claire's azure blue eyes. *Daniel, what are you doing? Ashley is dead and Claire is grieving.*

He began to march up Market Street to the governor's hotel, and found the governor and his men unloading the wagon. As he approached, the governor spotted him in the crowd.

"Daniel, my friend, where is Philippe?"

"He is a few blocks over. Please tell me, how is Claire doing?"

"She is fine," returned the governor. "Why?"

"You have not heard, have you?" Daniel searched into Persifor's eyes. "Ashley is dead. He fell against the side of the ship as he was disembarking. He hit his head and fell into the bay, and was dead by the time they pulled him out of the water."

A wildfire of agony spread across the creases of Persifor's face, and he said, "Oh, my God."

Daniel continued, "This is such a terrible turn of events. Philippe and I are leaving for the gold fields in the morning, please give our sympathy. I will contact you when we get settled. And Persifor, thank you for all you have done for Philippe and myself."

"You are my dear friend, Daniel, like a son. This is terrible news. We will persevere through this. Let me know if I can help you in any way."

They shook hands and Daniel turned and began sculpting his path through the mud while a constant parade of men passed in a blur. He thought to himself, *I am glad I spoke to Persifor, as they had not yet heard the news.*

When Daniel reentered the saloon, there sat Philippe, his eyes glazed from the whiskey, and the two women attached to each arm.

With a determined glance, Daniel said, "Sorry to interrupt the party, Philippe, but we must go."

With bewildered apprehension, Philippe said, "Benet, what is your rush, we just got here. Please sit down and let me introduce you to my friends."

"Philippe, I said now, grab your things, we're leaving." Daniel tossed coins onto the table, picked up his carpetbag and Philippe's lock box, and walked away. Philippe kissed the women, grabbed his carpetbag, and went off after his friend.

The two travelers checked into a small, moldy tent crammed with twenty sleeping cots, well worn with many stories and various belongings.

Philippe pleaded, "What has gotten into you, Benet? We have traveled for two months at sea, we've been here on land an hour and you want to leave?"

His brows furrowed, and with a disdainful tone he said, "We came for gold, not women and whiskey."

Philippe grew a wide grin on his flushed face, and he pronounced, "Ah, my friend, it is not gold you are rushing for. You are rushing away from Claire and the death of her beloved Ashley. Now you want her more than ever."

Daniel's face, shrouded on the precipice of thought, pondered the words of his friend and continued, "Yes, you are right, Philippe. So you see, we must leave in the morning."

"If you stay here, you may be searching for hope, not gold, and you must know that hope is a poor bed partner."

A man entered, his jackboots caked in mud, and his clothes worn and tattered. He interjected, "Where are you two greenhorns headed?"

"The gold fields," Daniel responded in a determined tone. His green eyes glared, flanked by his skin, which was stained by the sun and hard work and outlined with deep lines of history traveling across his forehead and cheekbones.

The man said, "I have two more questions for you: which gold field and how are you planning to get there?"

"In the morning we'll buy two horses and be off to the east," said Daniel.

"You, my friends, are either very rich or very naive, or perhaps both. Do you actually believe you are the only ones here trying to get to the gold fields by horse? If you can find a horse in this town, be ready to pay $1,000."

Both friends' faces clouded in dismay, and Daniel responded, "You're not serious?"

"May I suggest a boat across the bay, into the delta at Benicia, and there you will find a boarding house called Isabel's. Her family has a rancho to the east in Avion and her father will sell you some good horses cheap—that is, if he likes you. You will need equipment and it is expensive. I suggest that you procure it there as well. From there, find your way to Dry Diggins."

Daniel interjected, "Is that a town?"

"Well, lads, easterners would not call it a town, they would call it lawless chaos. In this place, you must be rough and be ready to stake a claim." The man stopped, let loose a raspy cough and passed gas at the same time, then continued, "And also rough enough and ready to defend it with your life. My name is Jackson Black, lads," and he reached out his callous hand, weathered and arthritic and said, "Welcome to California." As the trio all shook hands, the tent was consumed with foul air.

34

Life calls a tune, we dance.

—John Galsworthy

The next morning, heading down Market Street, they observed three young children, huddled together in a circle, harvesting with their wet fingertips, flakes of gold that surely had been dropped in the mud the evening before.

Smiling, Philippe slapped his friend on his back and said, "It looks pretty easy, my friend, I think we are going to be rich!"

"Don't be a fool, nothing is easy. Keep walking."

Philippe began to laugh and said, "Ah, yes, just like love, eh, my friend?"

Daniel gave his friend a friendly shove, as if to say, *stop it.* With the bay and its calm water lying before them, his mind flashed once again to the image of me upside-down in my beautiful dress from Paris.

That evening they walked into Isabel's and were greeted by an older woman, her black hair draping her shoulders and her breasts full and bulging from white muslin against her bronze skin.

"Amigos, Como esta?" she said and she placed two glasses of beer in front of them.

"Ah, muy bien, gracias. Muy cansado," Philippe responded graciously.

Daniel said, "I hope you speak English. I hate it when he talks Spanish."

"Yes, I do," she said, her lips inviting and warm with a sly smile.

"My name is Daniel, and a man named Jackson Black told us to come here and look for a woman named Isabel."

Philippe interrupted and said, "Señora, please allow me to introduce myself, I am Philippe, Philippe Galvez. I must say you are more beautiful than a spring flower."

"Save your talk for the saloon girls, Galvez," she said and brought her eyes back to Daniel. "Why has my friend sent you to me?"

"We are headed to the gold fields and he said that you and your father could help us with some horses and supplies."

"Let me bring you some food and we will talk."

She returned with pozole and three beers and listened to their story, which ventured well into the evening.

Isabel's father's rancho was five miles to the east in Avion, so they would have to wait for the stagecoach to arrive in the morning or walk, and walking was not a good option because of thieves. They decided to wait for the stage.

During the night, Daniel tossed in disjointed sleep. In a dream, he told me that I called to him, and when I came into view I was hanging upside-down, frozen in my own despair, calling his name, "Mr. Benet, where did you go? I need you to help me! How dare you leave me now! Where are you? Please cut me down." Daniel reached for me and then suddenly awoke, sweating profusely and overcome with a rippling sadness. A rooster in the distance cackled and the faint sound wrinkled back into the coming dawn, and Daniel fell back into a restless slumber.

The sun bloomed open a large sky with a calm stillness, permeating a fresh batch of hope. Philippe and Isabel played dominoes and drank coffee, and Daniel sat on the porch and sketched the terrain. His thoughts yielded to an image of Ashley, the large gash on his temple, bloodied and swollen, as he lay lifeless. Daniel felt his emotions falling over a cliff and he thought to himself, *My God, Claire must be so terribly devastated.* He stood up and looked in on the domino game, then said, "I'm taking a walk."

A half-hour later, forlorn and bags packed, Daniel stepped toward the domino game and announced, "I must go back to San Francisco, Claire needs me now."

Philippe, his eyes full and round, responded, *"Mon Dieu, mon ami, est-ce que vous vous êtes fou ? Il n'y a rien pour vous à San Francisco!"*

"Excuse me," declared Isabel as she bolted to her feet.

Daniel stood confused as his friend interpreted, "My God, my friend, have you gone crazy? There is nothing for you in San Francisco!"

"Philippe, your friend is in love, he has no other choice but to follow his heart." Isabel stood behind Philippe in baggy pantaloons, a jaunty black hat with silver disks, and a short embroidered bolero jacket.

With his eyes wide, searching hers for hope, Daniel said, "Isabel, I need a horse to the boat."

Isabel returned, relaxed, "My nephew Fernando will ride with you and bring back the horse. He will return next week to get supplies and can pick you up, will you be there?"

"I will do my best, Isabel, and thank you for everything, you are a kind woman."

"Okay, my friend," said Philippe. "I will wait for you at Isabel's father's rancho."

35

In Chinese, the word for crisis is wei ji,
composed of the character wei, which means danger,
and the character ji, which means opportunity.

—JAN WONG

The year was 1838, in Shanghai, China, and Chang Hui was a twenty-nine-year-old doctor specializing in trauma wounds, broken bones, skin and respiratory conditions, and dentistry. He had worked hard his whole life. At age sixteen, Chang left his family in Anhui province after a life of not being the number one son. Having respiratory problems, he was chided by his family as weak and unworthy. Chang's life changed forever on the day his lungs collapsed, restricting his airflow and rendering him unable to do his chores. In a fit of rage, his father began to beat him.

"Why are you so weak? You humiliate our family name. Why can't you be a man, do your work?" After a night of drinking and gambling, his father arrived home the next day announcing he had used his weak son in a bet and lost him. He boasted of how proud he was of himself, losing him to a doctor. "Perhaps he can get my son to work like a man."

Chang's mother fell, wailing in a swirling hysteria of grief, hitting her husband on his chest, screaming "No! No! No! Why? Why?

He is not your son he is mine. You do not deserve him! You are an animal!" He responded by knocking her unconscious to the floor.

The next day the doctor arrived and took Chang Hui away in his wagon, as Chang's mother watched her son and wailed in sadness.

She confronted her husband in front of her family, saying to him, "Zhi, you are the devil." From her apricot-yellow *jifu* dragon robe—made of the finest gauze weave silk with gold-wrapped thread embroidery in a fu design, which represented the power to judge— she revealed a carved ivory dagger, and she released the scabbard with her other hand. Her eyes slowly scanned her two sons and then her daughter then returned back to Zhi, her gaze clouded with hatred and disgust. She raised the blade to her throat, and ran the knife across her skin with imperious precision. Her blood spurted onto the stone patio, where she collapsed in a pool of her own blood and died.

Chang Hui became the property of Wu Shangxian, a prominent physician in the Provence. Chang worked with Wu for thirteen years, learning the art of healing. Wu became the loving father Chang never had. The painful memories of his father, along with the news of his mother's death and his lost siblings, settled into a dark, distant place, shrouded in a perpetual wasteland of melancholy, and though over time they lessened, they would never leave him, surfacing in his worst moments.

Chang learned the five treatments of Chinese medicine: treat the whole body, nourish the whole body, cure the spirit, give medications, and use acupuncture and massage. He learned how to reveal the causes of disharmony in a patient's body and act appropriately.

He studied and collected the five classes of medications: herbs, insects, trees, grains and stones, along with the curative minerals and metals. One medication, which proved most useful to Chang, was the use of ephedra, which he carried in a netsuke on his sash.

Chang was awakened, suddenly, late one evening by a young boy. He was told that Shangxian needed his assistance and to come quick with his doctor bags and all of the supplies he could carry. Without hesitation, Chang left with the boy, who took him to the waterfront, where they entered a fan-tan and were then greeted by three Tanka girls. They nuzzled into Chang as he struggled with his bags to push them away.

"Do not touch me with your filth, I have been called to treat a patient. Where is master Shangxian?"

One of the girls motioned toward the back room as a large man appeared from a door and said with a bow, "Welcome, Chang Hui, it is an honor and thank you for arriving so quickly at this hour." He held the curtain open for him to enter. Chang entered a dark, damp hallway that turned to the left and felt his lungs react to the smell as he saw Shangxian lying in a heap on the floor, bloodied and unconscious. As Chang began to turn he was struck hard on the back of his head with a blunt instrument, rendered unconscious. Chang awoke in a wagon, his hands tied and someone forcing something into his mouth. He began to struggle, but he knew immediately what was happening to him and fell unconscious again. The next day, he awoke and found himself feeling drugged and aboard an English sailing ship with no land in sight.

The ship's captain was James Fulbright, a huge man half a foot short of seven feet and almost that around his waist. He was weathered as an old boot, with a terrible limp and a heartbreaking cough.

Chang asked, "Why have you kidnapped me?"

"I did not kidnap you, Chang. I am in a terrible need of a doctor," Fulbright explained.

"Was it Shangxian who had me kidnapped?"

"No, he tried to protect you," Fulbright said. "Shangxian was drunk and lost playing cards, more than he could pay. The men were angry, so they beat him. They wanted to sell him to me, but unfortunately they beat him to death. They found a boy who knew of your location, so they found you to reclaim their money."

"I thought you might be Shangxian until a short while ago." Chang settled onto his haunches and began to weep large and sorrowful tears.

Fulbright was empathetic, but in great need of a doctor. "I am on a schedule and you are on my ship to Australia. It is a terribly unfortunate circumstance, yet a good thing is, you have your medical bags and they left you with your inheritance."

"My inheritance?"

Fulbright reached behind the cabin door and displayed Shangxian's medical bags.

Chang's heart leapt as he pulled them into his arms and brought Shangxian's scent to his grief.

His overwhelming sorrow for his master's demise and his unfortunate fate settled over time. Chang was vaguely familiar with the English language, as well as French, Portuguese, and Spanish, as he and Shangxian had serviced the shipping community for years. He preferred treating his countrymen, yet he was quite intrigued by the foreigners' wild tales of adventure and landscape. With no way of changing his fate, Chang accepted it with dignity and honor, and his acceptance did not go unnoticed by the captain. Chang treated the captain's aliments in exchange for lessons in English.

From Australia he traveled to New Zealand, Tahiti, Bora Bora, Cook Islands, Fiji, and then to Valparaiso, Lima, and finally Yerba Buena, where the Captain said he was going to sprout his land shoes. His friend from England was there and he talked of settling down with a Spanish maiden. Chang landed in Yerba Buena in the summer of 1840 and was released, a free man.

36

—CHINESE PROVERB

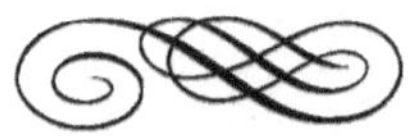

Since Ashley's demise, I moved through my world comatose and in woeful lamentation, as if floating upon a broken leaf, burdened with an agonizing guilt. I sit now, in a daze, in a high-backed mohair Regency rosewood chair, facing my second-floor window, while the street below bustles with life. The room is larger than my room on the *California,* and it's stunning compared to many other accommodations in the city's chaos. But all I can do is stare, as faint shades of color glower through the frame of glass.

March 8, 1849

Dearest Uncle,

This is a most difficult letter to write. My beloved Ashley is dead and my life appears to be evaporating as I write this to you. Not in my worst nightmares could I have imagined my present predicament. During our journey, Ashley had been ill, and the stress of the coal shortage and the resulting chaos just wore him down. I had suspected cholera, but he never got worse, just a low fever, headache, and dizzy spells. He insisted that I leave the *California* with the governor's party because he wanted to supervise the mail and our belongings and be the last one off with the captain. Apparently he became dizzy and collapsed as he was stepping off the ship, hitting his head and falling into the bay.

I feel gorged with guilt over my ill feelings toward Ashley. I realize I was being selfish and spoiled, always demanding so much of his attention when he carried such a burden of responsibility on his shoulders. You must know how hard it was for me to be sequestered on that ship for three months.

Oh, Uncle, how will I survive in this riotous city of mud and men! There are no laws and gambling, drinking and prostitution are rampant. I cannot leave my room for the fear of catcalls from mobs of drunken men who have forgotten what bathing is.

I am lost in a sea of confusion. I will not get back on a ship for another three or four months, nor will I take a stage to head east to Boston. That seems so very dangerous. I can't stay here, and I cannot leave. The Governor and his wife have been so gracious and supportive of me. I will stay with them into the spring and then I will come home to you and Watuppa Pond.

Love,

Claire

37

*Absence diminishes small loves and increases great ones,
as the wind blows out the candle and fans the bonfire.*

—Francois VI de la Rochefoucault

The next day, after another night of windblown rain, Daniel returned to a San Francisco that sat under huge pillow clouds cloaked by blue sky and a brisk wind. As he walked briskly down the wharf, Daniel's mind wandered back to his memories of our meeting in the forest. *What are you doing, Benet,* he said to himself, *she's mourning the loss of her husband. She does not want to see you, at least certainly not alone.* With that thought, Daniel decided to ask the governor his thoughts on the matter.

Beads of sweat percolated his forehead as he knocked on the governor's door, and a moment later the governor's wife, Ellen, appeared.

"Mr. Benet, what a surprise, how are you doing?" she said. "I thought you and Mr. Galvez left for the gold fields? The governor is not in, may I help you?"

"It is true, we did, but I've returned. I'm worried about Claire. She must be just devastated with Ashley's passing. What will she do without him?"

Ellen replied, "Claire is surviving, barely. She has slipped into a deep depression. We are all praying for her health. She has requested no visitors. She even turned away Goldie and Frances. You know, these things take time."

With a swell of hope, he pulled a letter from his shirt. "Could you please see that she gets this? I only wish her the best."

Ellen searched Daniel's blue eyes then took the letter from him.

"Thank you, Ellen, for all you and the governor have done for both Philippe and myself."

"You are both good men and I know that the governor thinks highly of you both."

Rubbing his arm, glancing into the room over her shoulder, Daniel began to fidget with his coat, and backed away, saying, "Well, I should be going. Please give the governor my best and also to Claire." With a tip of his hat, he turned and nodded back to her and said, "Good day."

He stepped off the boardwalk into the mud, as a mangy dog searched for scraps in the street. As he throttled through the mud up Washington Street, he saw a pair of rats scamper along the plank boards leading to Portsmouth Plaza. As he entered a gambling hall called the El Dorado, his senses were overloaded with choking cigar smoke and sounds, boisterous and large, as scantily clad woman prowled the drunken crowd with hope. Benet found a seat and ordered a porterhouse steak with baked apples, lima beans, fried potatoes, and a mammoth glass of Mason Celebrated Beer. After his food arrived, a fledgling of a man approached, pulled out his pistol, and pointed it at Daniel Benet.

"This here is the man who robbed me of my gold the night before last," he shouted to the crowd in a gravelly voice, his face dancing, mottled with a whiskey glaze.

Daniel returned his gaze and said, "You are mistaken, my friend, as I have only arrived this afternoon from Benicia."

"You are a thief and a liar, step into the street, ya bloke, or I'll shoot you dead where you sit."

At this moment, the man sitting across from Daniel set his fork onto his plate of pork chops and applesauce and adjusted his pants as he stood. With the force of a winter storm, he backhanded the drunken man with his pistol, breaking the man's nose and knocking him backward to the floor, bleeding profusely. The gambling hall drew a hushed silence. A woman's unrestrained laughter ruptured the moment, and the air hovered thick in quiet anticipation. The gentleman, now standing over Daniel's accuser, was larger than any man he had ever seen.

"Like the gentleman said, you have made a mistake, he just arrived from Benicia. Now leave or I will drag your battered carcass into the mud and beat you to a pulp."

Wobbly and dazed, the man left the El Dorado, and the room slowly returned back to its raucous life as if nothing had happened.

With a deep breath and wide eyes, Daniel now looked across at the bear of a man and said, "I owe you one, sir, my name is Benet, Daniel Benet."

The huge stranger winked at a saloon girl and said, "Bring my friend and me another round." As the man turned back to his pork chop, Daniel fixed upon his eyes of marbled malachite. "No problem, Mr. Benet," he said as his hand reached across the table. Daniel's hand submerged into his grip, he continued, "I am Jacob Bradley. I can't stand these pesky little mosquitoes fevered with greed and revenge, fueled by alcohol and a pistol, accusing anyone of their own misfortune." Bradley continued eating and then said, "So what brings you from Benicia?"

He looked at his plate of food and then back to Jacobs's malachite gaze, and said, "A woman."

Bradley erupted into a turbulent roll of laughter, bouncing with joyful intent as Daniel, now awkwardly flushed, retreated to his plate. After a few more chuckles, Bradley looked around the room and continued, "Yes, my friend, you and five thousand more of us!"

By the end of his meal, Daniel had summed up his journey, and as Bradley ordered more beers, Daniel asked, "How about you?" And with that Bradley began his tale.

"I made it up to the saw mills at Sutter's fort and procured employment. After a short time, I met some good, trusting men, Joe White, Malcolm, Lacrosse, and McPhail. Everyone had heard how Weber Creek had gold and it was found in much greater loads than anywhere. Weber's Creek is a small tributary to the northern fork of the Americano River, so of course we were determined to undertake the journey. Upon arriving to the small valley, which drained the stream called Weber Creek, there was quite a camp there, yet not to the size of, say, Mormon diggings. The whole valley is speckled over with tents and arbors of green brush and the creek was spread with miners, sifting, digging, and washing. We decided to follow a group of Mormons, who had left one week prior to Bear River, which flows into the Sacramento River, fifty miles to the north. On surveying the Bear River country, we found ourselves in a wild land—no natives, far less a white man, were to be seen. We traveled the distance of eight miles or so, negotiating some of the main tributaries of the main river, and had the good fortune to land upon a spot, and we found that gold existed in abundance in the sand and shingles, which were imbedded in flakes amid the rocks."

Daniel interjected, "My God, Bradley, what luck!"

"The next day, while several of us were rambling about the neighborhood of the camp, exploring the several canyons laid before us, we found, among the slack rock that had crumbled away from the sides of the ravine and fallen to the bottom, several nuggets of gold, of a much larger size than any we had yet discovered. This seduced us to explore the upper part of the ravine, where favorable traces of gold were easily detected. With further examination we were convinced that gold existed here to a much greater extent than anywhere we had been working. After working only a few hours, we were successful in attaining more gold than we had taken in any days during the past weeks."

"You have had good fortune, Jacob."

Bradley leaned across the table and cawed as his fist and fork hit the table. "My story is not over, Benet! After two weeks, we all decided to cash in and head to the coast to San Francisco. Malcolm had the strongest horse, so we agreed that he should carry the bulk of the gold, which we had figured to be fifty pounds."

Daniel interjected, "My God, fifty pounds!"

"Joe White and myself filled our saddlebags at twenty-eight pounds each and were to form a guard for protection from Indians and highwaymen. Lacrosse and McPhail held over twenty pounds in their bags.

As the new day withered the darkness to light, we began our descent out of the canyons to Sutter's Fort. We had agreed to have two riders in front and three in the back, with Joe White on one side and myself on the other of Malcolm. The birds were feeding and calling from the low hills, as the brush was thick and groves of oaks, sycamores, and pines painted the draws, their leaves tickled at the sky in a slight breeze. As we entered a draw of oaks mixed with Jack pines, we came into a glade, and no animal sounds to break the silence. Thinking back, I now realize we should have noticed, but we didn't. At this time, Malcolm's horse paused to defecate. Unknowingly, Joe White and I sauntered forward to a halt. As I turned around to check on Malcolm, the morning sun coming over the rise blinded my vision as a howling scream rose out of the woods. An Indian bolted out of the cover on horseback and lassoed Malcolm and yanked him off his horse. Three white men thrust out at Malcolm's horse and began to chase it in the opposite direction. Lacrosse and McPhail drew their pistols and fired at the attackers, but they were gone from the glade and chasing Malcolm's horse back into the hills. Joe White and I bolted after them, yet soon realized that with all of the cover we were an easy ambush, and returned to our friends. Malcolm was unconscious for a period of time and had a broken arm and some ribs. In a matter of moments we lost a good portion of two weeks of hard work."

Daniel sat stunned at the story's outcome. He said, "That is a sad tale, my friend."

Bradley's eyes pierced his gaze across the table once again and he said, "Let me just say, young man, that you have been counseled on what you seek to attempt. For every nugget you find, there are ten men ready to steal it from you and they will not think twice to kill you for it as well."

"What happened to Malcolm? Has he recovered?"

"We took Malcolm into Sacramento and left him in the care of a Chinaman named Chang. He is quite well known on I Street in Sacramento, he carries a netsuke on his sash, inlayed with mother-of-pearl. He was a doctor in China and was shanghaied on a ship, about ten years ago. He ended up in San Francisco and he practices his craft in Sacramento, but I think he plays cards mostly."

"What is a netsuke?"

"He has some trouble breathing apparently and he carries his medicine in the pouch on his sash for when he has a fit with breathing."

Daniel laid that night revisiting Jacob's haunting story over and over. He now wondered if he was actually willing to risk his life in the search for gold. And what would happen to me? He was still pondering my fate as he drifted to sleep.

******

Thinking out loud, Brodie questioned, "People stole stuff and attacked people, killed them for their gold?"

"That's right, Brodie, just like pirates," added Maeve.

"I think pirates were bad people," Brodie continued.

"Chickabiddies, there have always been bad people," Grammy interjected.

"And there always will be," added Vanessa.

"What was that saying I used to say to you and Emily?" Grammy's eyes were full and clear, searching into her melting past.

"'Girls, you must always be aware of what is unfolding before you. It will keep you safe.' That one?"

With a loving smile, Grammy said, "Chickabiddies, your mother is a smart woman."

Grammy looked at Vanessa in a new way now. The years of love given and rarely felt or returned had given Vanessa such a jaded opinion about her grandmother that it clouded this moment. Yet the sky had somehow cleared, in a way that she still did not quite understand.

38

If your teeth are clenched and your fists are clenched
your life span is probably clenched.

—Adabelia Radici

Daniel's journey across the bay back to Benicia lengthened when the boat captain ran aground at low tide during the night and they had to wait eight hours to get free from the bay mud. Upon arriving, Daniel saw Isabel's nephew Fernando Pacheco.

"Buenos días, Daniel. Como estás?" Fernando said.

"Good morning Fernando," responded Daniel.

Fernando continued, "My Tía Isabel was called away, as my cousin Marta is birthing her first child. She has asked me to help you in any way I can on your journey to Salvio's rancho. It is where your friend Mr. Galvez is waiting."

By late afternoon, Daniel and Philippe sat under a massive oak tree drinking beer as Philippe listened to Jacob Bradley's tale from the gold fields.

"My friend, it appears that gold is easy to find, yet difficult to hang on to. Perhaps we need to come up with a few plans. But first, you must share your encounter with Mrs. Ashley."

"I was hoping you would not ask, with the continued threat of your incessant teasing." Daniel's face narrowed into a sheepish grin.

"I did not see her, because she has sequestered herself in her room. I spoke with Ellen, and she told me Claire has drifted into a deep depression and that these things take time to wash out. I gave her my letter and left. She has been commissioned a terrible fate, Philippe."

As the winter sun waned and its palette ignited hues of burnt vermillion to the west, the two Argonauts planned their journey to Dry Diggins and beyond.

39

Strong lives are motivated by dynamic purposes.

—Kenneth Hildebrand

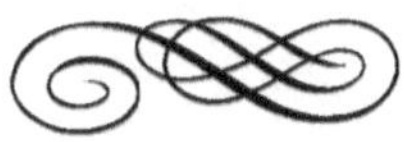

March 15, 1849

Claire,

My heart aches for the loss of your beloved Ashley. This most unfortunate occurrence is a dreadful reminder that our lives can change at any moment. It is my hope that you can shun your sadness from this tragedy soon.

I wish to apologize to you for my annoying behaviors while aboard the *California*. My actions toward you were never with malicious intent. I cannot really explain what happened that day on the Boston Post Road, or how, and perhaps more important, why we found ourselves on the *California* together for those weeks. What I do know is, I am remorseful for making you feel uncomfortable, as that was not ever my intent. I hope that you can bring yourself to forgive me. Philippe and I are on our way to the gold fields. In Benicia, we met a woman named Isabel who runs a boarding house, and she took us in for a few days.

She has kindly offered to receive our mail. We procured horses and supplies from her father, who lives nearby. We have heard many disheartening tales of backbreaking work, expensive food, robbery, and murder. Despite such tales, we are pressing on to the foothills to a town called Dry Diggins.

Your loss of Ashley must be so terribly sorrowful, but with time your heartache will hopefully pass. I worry about you in such a raucous place as San Francisco without Ashley's protection. I wish you the best, Claire.

Fondly,

Daniel

Still holding the letter, I sat in the Regency chair, my eyes gazing into a blurred space, as a spring rain lightly fell on Portsmouth Plaza. As if frozen in some forgotten time, my body was trapped in a sheer muslin day dress, tinted with a floral wreath of roses wrapped with ivy leaves and tendrils.

My hands glided tenderly onto my lap, as the bishop sleeves of my dress draped the letter. Floating images of Ashley's smile, warm and secure, radiated in my thoughts, but in my depression I was swimming, reaching for some kind of attention, unfocused and yet clear. I saw my hand in slow motion, slapping Daniel, the mud spitting into the colors of the forest. My reverie shifted and then crashed, as the steel spar shattered my piano, and Daniel and Philippe protected my honor—then to Ashley coughing, consumed in a feverish doom. My mind wandered, lost in the moment, and the letter fell to the floor as I began to release large, sorrowful sobs, bruised by my agony.

******

Vanessa stopped reading and sat up, realigning herself, and drew in a shallow but mindful breath. "My goodness, Claire is a mess. She is wobbling in one world and then into the next. Will this woman ever find happiness?"

Brodie consoled her. "Mom, she just lost her husband. Of course she is sad. Grammy, you must have been very sad when your husband died."

Grammy looked over the top of her glasses said, "Yes, that is true, Brodie, I was terribly sad and I turned into cold, bitter woman. I almost drowned in my own self-pity. Yet usually in the end, most people find their own happiness. Finding happiness is surviving. You three are my happiness."

Maeve and Brodie's faces swelled with pride. Vanessa, returning to her thoughts, was greeted by a surging epiphany. *Did Grammy ever think she was like Claire?*

40

It is the possibility that keeps me going, not the guarantee.

—NICOLAS SPARKS

Daniel and Philippe were finally on their new tramp with fresh horses, supplies, and a Mexican mule to carry them. Philippe joked, "We should call him Sir Frederick, after the drunkard who vomited into the wind on the *Falcon.*"

"Why, because he was such an ass?" questioned Daniel.

"Well, that too. Do you remember when he said that he carried the weight of God? Well, if you can carry the weight of God, you should be pretty strong, right? So Sir Frederick is going to carry our fortune."

"Philippe, what was the name of your last horse?"

"His name was Henry, yours?"

"Buttons. I miss that horse. I hated giving him up friend in New York."

"I miss Henry as well, I left him with my mother, but who knows if I will ever return," Philippe said sadly.

"Of course you will, when we strike it rich. We will travel first class!"

With a tempered sigh, Philippe said, "I am naming my horse Henry."

With a jovial sigh, Daniel responded, "Well, Henry, meet Buttons."

They crossed the river by ferry to Benicia, and set off to the northeast through the tules. Then up through live oaks and up rolling hills, and they got their first view of their journey toward the east. Flanked on either side, they were bathed in a vibrant spring of green, as red-winged black birds darted through the sky and busily collected materials for their spring nests.

After several moments of silence Philippe said, "I never realized that California had her own Mississippi. Now I understand why Salvio said to follow the low hills to the left of the delta. Do you know what Sacramento means in Spanish?"

"No, tell me."

"'Holy sacrament.' We have a long journey, look at the mountains and all of the snow."

"That has to be over a hundred miles away. Those are the highest mountains I have ever seen," added Daniel.

Prompting his horse to move, Philippe turned back, smiling, and said, "So what are you waiting for?"

"I am waiting for you to get out of the way," Daniel teased, as he tugged at Sir Frederick. The mule snorted in frustration and passed gas before moving.

That first day, the men traveled thirty miles and celebrated their first meal with fresh pheasant and rabbit. They had encountered game in abundance in the marshlands, coming upon herds of elk, antelope, and deer, but decided taking one would be a waste of meat. As they bunked under a massive white oak, millions of stars twinkled through ancient, gnarled limbs, and the two friends pondered their eastward journey into the wild unknown.

41

We make our road by walking.

—Paulo Freire

The morning rose from the east as the horses snorted and stomped for water and grass and their nostrils flared against a crisp blanket of spring frost sparkling shards of light against the rising sun. As they gathered grass for the horses Daniel and Philippe agreed to head out without a fire, so as the horses ate, they ate cold tamales given to them by Isabel's mother.

Around mid-morning, the road twisted down into a sprawling sea of tules and willow, and at times Philippe thought he was back home in the swamps. His story began with his parents, both of whom were French; his mother was also Spanish. Philippe was born an only child off the coast of Mexico and Texas, in his father's compound. He never met his father, but knew that his name was Jean Laffite and he was a privateer and a businessman. That was a family secret he would take to his grave. Daniel remembered that his father had spoken of a man named Laffite, who helped Andrew Jackson during the Battle of New Orleans in 1812.

Daniel said, "Philippe, you are famous!"

Philippe's brows creased, and his jaw stiffened, and with a sharp tone he said, "I was named after an island for a reason, Benet. My parents wanted my identity to be unknown for a reason, and you will too."

Daniel fell silent and chewed on his friend's words for a long while.

After a long silence Philippe continued, "I mean it, Benet!"

"I know that, Philippe, and your secret will die with my death. You are my trusted famous friend and business partner," he chided.

"Daniel, please stop! I am serious!"

By noon they were ankle-deep in their jackboots, leading the horses as the redwings danced in shades of green, and soon they began to come out of the tules and willows. They fed and rested the horses on a broad tabletop of majestic groves of sycamores, cottonwoods, and oaks, standing regal along the Sacramento River, while eating beef jerky and cold tamales.

By noon the next day the men completed the first leg of their tramp as they arrived at the convergence of the Sacramento and Americano Rivers in the Embarcadero of Sacramento. Geographically, Sacramento was absent of San Francisco's hills, but it bustled with sprawling tents and men from around the world. The fever of gold loomed a frenzied bubble over the city. They celebrated their journey with a trip to the bathhouse, a hot meal, beers, and a good cigar.

"You know, Daniel, this California is a lot like Louisiana," Philippe said.

"How so, Galvez?" Daniel asked.

"The river, the water, the endless water, the marshes and bogs, and the flooding. *Este es un lugar estúpido para un pueblo!*" Philippe said.

"Can we try that one more time?"

"This is a stupid place for a town, you just can't put a town on the flood plain where two rivers meet! Eventually this town will be washed away."

"You sound like a politician," Daniel chided.

"I sound like your friend, Daniel. Let's find us a poker game and a drink."

"I am tired, Philippe, and am going to check the horses and Frederick. Perhaps I should write to my mother."

"And Claire?" coaxed Philippe.

"And so what if I do?"

"Benet, all I am saying is, if you love her, and I believe you do, then you should continue to contact her. If your communication is unwanted, she will tell you, believe me."

"Yes, Claire would do that, wouldn't she?"

Back at the stable, the stable attendant was absent but Daniel found everything intact. He decided to stay with the horses and Sir Frederick and found his writing book, a candle, and a stool. Sitting in the shadowy light, he lit a cigar and pondered where to begin.

March 21, 1849

Claire,

As I am writing this letter to you I am merely a jumble of emotions. I cannot explain all that has happened. You must be saddened in your mournful grief. I have been both saddened and humbled by Ashley's demise. My heart breaks for your terrible mountain of sorrow. In time, you will heal, Claire, and your life will get better. Death shrouds us daily, lingering in the shadows, and never forgets. Ashley will always be a part of you.

I cannot explain what happened in the forest that day. A truly unique set of circumstances, and those brief moments we shared together have had a powerful effect on my life since. Your beauty captured my heart the moment I looked into your eyes, and then I knew that I was captured for life. Your unyielding and tenacious spirit hooked me line and sinker. I cannot get you out of my thoughts, after all of this time. Being with you on the *California* was a prison I never imagined, and yes, I know it was disruptive for both of us. It was painful for me to not be able to share my heart with you.

Fondly,

Daniel

42

The path of sound credence is the thick forest of skepticism.

—George Kean Nathan

Philippe stepped onto the boardwalk with coins in his hand and began to knock the side of the walk with his jackboots, spattering mud precariously back into the street. Looking up, as flies danced around horse droppings, he caught a glimpse across the street of three brown-eyed girls, who giggled as he sent a smile in their direction. A small boy painted in filth, his face spotted with sores, asked to shine his jackboots.

Philippe moved his jackboot away and said, "No, thank you, son."

Inside the saloon, Philippe found himself immersed with all of humanity, in an intoxicated, smoke-filled haze. As his eyes adjusted, they met the contemplation of a woman. She approached him with complete control and purpose, and stopped inches from his face, as French lavender permeated the air between them. She said her name was Marie and she was fresh in town. She had raven hair, a ruffled dress, a necklace made of gold, and all the French perfume you'd care to smell.

"Hello, young lady. How did you know I love French perfume? I'm pleased to make your acquaintance, Marie. I'm Philippe Galvez. I am hoping to find an honest card game."

"There is one, if you don't mind playing with a Chinaman."

The tent was wet and mildewed, and cigar smoke hovered above. She led him to the back of the tent to a partitioned room where a Chinaman sat at a card table of birds-eye maple inlaid with abalone florets. His long ponytail was tucked behind his loose-fitting, colorful jacket.

He stood and bowed and said, "Greetings, traveler, where are you from?"

"New Orleans. How about you?"

"I am from Shanghai."

Behind him was a young Indian woman, perhaps nineteen or twenty. She stood stout and proud, wearing some sort of apron of maple bark, fore and aft with strips of buckskin decorated with deer hooves, pine nuts, and abalone. Her presence flooded the small room as Philippe sank into the moment. Her ears bore plugs, which were bone of pelican with charcoal designs and inlaid with abalone. She wore a flat top winter hat of shredded tule, woven with hazel shoots, bear grass, and maidenhair fern, all in a full and twisted overlay of shells. Her moccasins and leggings were of deer hide with fur on the inside. On her chin, a tattoo of three lines, from her lower lip to her chin, from the charcoal of nutmeg. Her eyes pierced Philippe, which made him feel uneasy.

"Mind if I join your game? I am Philippe Galvez."

Chang bowed. "Welcome Mr. Galvez, I am Chang Hui, a curator of medicine and life-long health. Let me introduce you to my assistant, Kome Pano Yeponi, Moon Bear Spirit Doctor. I will warn you, she is my good luck charm. It has been said that what she dreams, comes true."

Philippe warbled a frail, timid laugh and sat down. The young woman's eyes, wide and enticing, tracked his every movement. Marie returned and moved in close to Galvez, sliding his beer close as she sipped a shot of whiskey.

Philippe asked, "Do you know a man named Malcolm with an injured arm?"

Chang, now puzzled, asked, "How do you know this man named Malcolm and why do you ask me this?"

"I was told he was taken to a Chinese doctor who carried a netsuke on his sash, inlayed with mother-of-pearl." Chang's eyes glistened like the stars and he nodded as he clutched his netsuke in one hand. As they played cards Philippe told Daniel's story of Bradley and Malcolm. Philippe lost the first two hands, won the third, then lost the next seven.

As his brows collapsed, Philippe said to Moon Bear, with a humorous glance, "What about my luck?"

"Your luck is your own, swim up river strong like the salmon. Just leap into the falls." Her look transcended time and space and Philippe felt free. *One more game,* he thought, still pondering losing nine of ten hands. He was ready to head back to the stable and Benet, yet Moon Bear's eyes held him with intent and reverie. In his head he heard, *Just do it,* and Philippe gestured to Chang for one more deal.

"You have faith, Mr. Galvez, a good trait in life, which helps to balance your chi."

Looking at his cards, Philippe saw that he held only two kings, and he asked for three more cards. As each card appeared, his heart anticipated the win: two aces and a deuce, the wild card. Philippe's eyes found Moon Bear's gaze, trancelike and euphoric, and as she shyly smiled at him, he sipped his beer and pondered the moment, full and complete.

Chang, his body at rest and filled with calm, stated, "I call you, Mr. Galvez."

Philippe laid each card, one at a time, his eyes piercing Moon Bear's eyes deeply.

Chang, with a gentle nod, noble and elegant, said, "Such a powerful finish, Mr. Galvez."

"Thank you for the game, my new friend, I must meet with my partner as we are leaving for the gold fields in the morning."

"Best wishes on your tramp for gold, Mr. Galvez. If you ever need my help I will offer you my best."

With a gentlemanly nod Philippe said, "Thank you, Chang, Moon Bear." At the mention of her name, Moon Bear bowed like Chang, and her smile left the imprint of the moment on him.

Galvez got up to leave and Marie, her eyes shimmering, said, "Well, Mr. Galvez, what shall we do now?"

"Thank you for your company, Marie, but I must go."

****

"Mom," Brodie asked, "what did they call Philippe's father?"

"Do you mean 'privateer?'" Vanessa said.

"Yeah."

"Jean Laffite was famous, and some called him a pirate. He was French and was from New Orleans."

Grammy said, "There're many tall tales about Mr. Laffite and what happened to him. His life has been shrouded in mystery."

Maeve asked, "Do you mean nobody knows what happened to him?"

"That is about it, sugar pop," Grammy said.

"I bet he left buried treasure. All pirates bury their treasure," Brodie added.

"Many, many people have had that same thought, little man, but no treasure has ever been found, at least not that anyone has ever declared." Grammy's eyes were wide and mysterious.

Glancing at her Grammy, Vanessa thought—*Now along with a treasure box, there's a pirate in the family! Why did she keep this from me?*

43

There's nowhere you can be that isn't where you're meant to be.

—JOHN LENNON

Kome Pano Yeponi was born in 1830. Her mother was a Miwok, and her father Maidu. Born Kome Pano, Moon Bear was raised by her father, a shaman, after her mother died from malaria in an epidemic brought on by fur trappers, which killed an estimated two thirds of the area's native population. By 1840, those who had survived were displaced from their ancestral villages as the establishment of towns pushed the few remaining groups to remote village sites.

Moon Bear was her father's one happiness, and he took her everywhere and taught her all the stories of the ancestors, the animals, and the plants. Most of all, he helped guide her path, to find her gifts of dream power and to summon spirit helpers in healing the energy of human nature and illness.

When Moon Bear was fourteen, she and her father took a five-day walk to Golden Sun Mountain Pool. It was Ném-diâkâm-pâkâm, "Big Moon," when all fruits ripen, that she had her first dreaming.

Her father stood next to her and said, "You must always believe in yourself. I have brought you to this spirit place to find your purpose."

"What am I to do, Father?"

"You are to dive into the pool to find your purpose."

Not understanding, Moon Bear dove off a boulder into the center of the pool. The water began to churn and bubble, yet she continued toward a light that shown like the sun at the bottom of the pool, and tobacco leaves begin to swim with her in the water. She reached for them, but they appeared to be too far away to grasp.

She surfaced and her father said, "Dive again, Moon Bear, you must grab at something. Perhaps you will catch something or perhaps not. If it goes well, you might grab something drifting in the pool."

Once more Moon Bear dove into the pool, toward the bright sunlight. She grabbed and caught a stone charm and held it in her hand, showing her father.

"This is good, my daughter, it is a gambling charm. You will always fare well in the grass game. You will secretly throw your bones into the grass with success! Your spirit is strong; you have been given a good sign on this test for power. You will transcend me, Moon Bear, you have great power."

44

*The bird that would soar above the level plain of tradition
and prejudice must have strong wings.*

—KATE CHOPIN

Sutter was a malevolent despot to the Indians. At the end of a day's labor, they were placed in holding pens or locked in rooms. The Indians were forced to sleep on the earthen floor, with no sanitary arrangements. The holding pens, after several weeks, were consumed with a squalid odor. The nocturnal incarceration was not agreeable to the Indians, which was obvious. Therefore, large numbers of natives ran away during the daytime. Many died for their actions. Moon Bear's father was one who ran each time he could. Sutter would send his posse to track him down and each time he was caught, he was usually whipped to unconsciousness. While being whipped for the last time, in front of Moon Bear, he was killed, after being hit in the back of the head with a hammer, as her screams drifted like smoke in the wind.

Moon Bear dreamed of her escape from Sutter every night, after working in Sutter's home all day. Then, one day, Moon Bear saw a Chinaman named Chang arrive at the fort. Sutter had summoned Chang, to treat an inflammation near his eyes. Even though Chang was Chinese, his services were very much welcomed by the

Americans, because doctors were hard to come by. Moon Bear's whole body filled with power, as the Chinaman in her dreams, was now here to take her away from certain death. Moon Bear knew four things that would happen next: he would take her away from Sutter, and he would protect her from harm, and he would keep her safe, and then she would be free.

As Chang opened his bag and began to organize his herbs, Moon Bear entered the room like a fresh breeze, bringing warm water and clean linens. She was dressed in white muslin, a sign of compliance for a girl her age.

Her eyes of raw umber met Chang's, as she placed a sprig of wormwood next to his satchel and stepped away. Chang straightened his torso, brought the sprig to his nose for a smell, and returned her gaze.

"You have powerful medicine, child."

Hearing Sutter coming down the hall, she put her hand to her mouth and Chang responded with a bow. As Chang examined his patient, Moon Bear asked if she was needed further, as she had to complete her morning chores. Sutter told her to leave.

While Chang began to mix his herbs in his mortar and pestle, he said, "I am making you a salve, John, it will reduce the inflammation. You must keep it out of your eyes, so do not rub it with your hands," Chang instructed.

"What do I owe you, Doc?"

"I have a business proposition for you, John. I am in need of an assistant that I can train to collect my herbs," Chang said.

"Yes, I see. So what do you have in mind?"

"I would like to purchase one of your Indians, the young girl, the one who brought in the water and clean linens."

"That girl will bolt on you like a wild horse, just like her father."

"And where is he, John?"

"He is dead."

"And your price for her?"

"I would be taking your money, that girl will run on you."

"I am willing to buy her before she runs on you, John, and that is a chance I am willing to take."

"I could fetch close to $200 for the girl in Sacramento."

"I will give you $100 and my services for the day, as I am already here."

"You have yourself a deal, Mr. Chang."

The two men shook hands and Sutter said, "I have two bad horses and my smithy has a bad burn. I want you to also check a couple of men for the measles."

Chang bowed and said, "I will do what I can."

As they left the fort, Chang tied Moon Bear to a rope, and she followed behind his horse. Chang assured her it was for her safety. Although he was well known for his ability to heal, he also was known to be honest and an example of the highest integrity. He needed her to look like his slave, as being Chinese was a danger to himself as well.

"What is your name, young lady?"

"My name is Kome Pano Yeponi."

"Does it have a meaning? Chinese names also have meaning."

"My name means Moon Bear Spirit Doctor."

"And this is why you gave me your herbs?"

"I gave you my herbs because I dreamed you. I am a Maidu shaman, like my father, dreaming is what I do. I had to leave that barbarian Sutter, so I called to you in my dreams, I brought you to me, and I am now with you and not Sutter. John Sutter is a vile man and he never realized that I am stronger than him."

"I believe you, Kome Pano Yeponi. We will be partners."

"I am aware of that, Chang," Moon Bear said, a sly smile bending, "I dreamed that too. Tell me what your name means?"

"My name is Chang Hui, it means wise old one."

"Yes, I know that, I dreamed you, remember?"

45

Love, Mercy, and Grace, sisters all,
attend your wounds of silence and hope.

—ABERJHANI

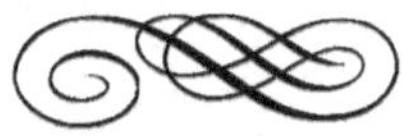

Daniel and Philippe awoke with a start as Sir Frederick's snorts shattered the early light. Getting up to check the animals, a heavy frost shrouding everything, Daniel saw Sir Frederick romping off behind a man on horseback.

"Hey!" Daniel shouted.

Daniel and Philippe saddled up and were on the chase five minutes later. Daniel yelled to his friend, "This is one crazy place we landed in, Galvez."

Philippe shouted back, "These men are drunken wild animals!"

They followed the tracks through the morning and beyond. At high noon, they entered a glade surrounded by oaks, madrone, and Jack pines and there was Sir Frederick grazing, with a saddled horse, grazing close by as well. On the ground lay a man about thirty years old, dead. Apparently he had been thrown off his horse and had hit his head on a large boulder, which was now painted with his blood.

Galvez laughed and said, "Looks like California justice."

"Back-handed justice," retorted Daniel.

They filtered through his things and found $4,000 and about ten ounces of nuggets. Daniel and Philippe worked quickly, took what they wanted, and left him, his horse, and his few supplies. Five minutes later the friends headed east toward Dry Diggins with Sir Frederick in tow, and didn't look back.

Our path is unplanned and our path is unknown.
Yet our journey is made whole when we travel as one.

—ANONYMOUS

April 18, 1849
Dearest Uncle,

Since my last letter I have gone from the depths of despair to the seemingly endless boundaries of my loneliness. I so miss you and Levi and Watuppa Pond. At times I wonder, will I ever see you again? Yet I know that I must move forward with my life, as you have taught me living is hard work that must be treasured. Persifor and his wife have been so terribly kind and helpful, they got me through some very rough times and I am lucky to have come out on the other side of this depression I have fallen into. It is unfortunate that they will be leaving for Monterey to attend the statehood convention soon and I will be on my own in this vile edge of civilization. Everything we brought with us is going into storage for its safety. My plan is to travel by ship to Benicia across the bay, where I will meet a woman named Isabel, and she will assist me in getting some employment. San Francisco is not safe for a woman on her own. I do hope to eventually receive my share of Ashley's estate, which being a woman, I know will not be much. I am hoping that you could help negotiate my portion with his family for me, as I am greatly in need of funds. I am sure that you have heard that prices are well over one hundred times higher than in Boston. Well, enough of poor me for now. You are in my loving thoughts, my dear uncle.

Love,

Claire

April 21, 1849

Dearest Mother,

Philippe and I have arrived in a town called Dry Diggins, the last outpost on the edge of this wild frontier. There are about two thousand men and ten women, seven of which are whores. This place is a sea of drunkards, gamblers, highwaymen, and convicts. Foreigners, Negroes, and the natives are bullied and abused and there are no laws enforced. I saw a man proven guilty in the street by a mob, fevered in liquor, and then hung by his neck at the nearest tree. It is by far the lowest stench of humanity you could imagine.

The countryside is a rolling blanket of green, as spring has arrived. This country called California cradles a landscape that is beautifully wild and pristine. I am pretty sure we have seen the last of the frost for the season, which is welcomed. Food is exorbitantly expensive and barely palatable. We are sleeping at our claim in a lean-to, as are the men in the surrounding claims. They are decent church going men and we look out for one another. We go in for supplies one claim at a time, so the others can protect the claim from being taken over by marauders. We struck it rich before we even got here. We came upon a dead man who had fallen off his horse somehow and hit his head on a boulder. He had $4,000 and ten ounces of nuggets, which is about another $350.

It is very dangerous to travel. We were told that for every honest man there are ten men willing to rob you or even kill you for your valuables. It is a raucous frontier of lawlessness, and violent men, and the mining is hard work. We have claimed a spot in a nearby ravine and we fill buckets of soil and attach them to Sir Frederick, our mule, and then haul the load to the stream to filter the nuggets out of the soil. I have found it easier to fill two half buckets rather than one full bucket for proper balance down the ravine.

I crave your corn pone, and of course those biscuits of yours and your bacon gravy. One could make a fortune selling your food to the hooligans, probably more money than you could get mining for gold. The real money here is in the selling of goods, not the gold.
With love,
Daniel

47

No one is so brave that he is not disturbed by something unexpected.

—Julius Caesar

Daniel and Philippe, after spending months together, finally discovered that their birthdays were ten days apart. Daniel's was May 10 and Galvez's May 20, so they decided to head down to Sacramento, primarily to deposit their money into a bank. The threat of being robbed was just too high a risk.

The two left the ravine at daybreak for the forty-mile ride to Sacramento. Dark, rolling clouds greeted them in the distance from the northwest, while the rising sun from the east cast its shadow ahead of them. By noon the coming storm was upon them and the wind whipped furiously through the trees as they entered a small meadow swale, which had served as a camping spot, with a fire ring of boulders. Suddenly the wind stopped, as if the world paused; the silence swallowed the moment. Henry paused and let out a snort as he pounded his left front hoof and took a few steps back. Philippe tried to steady the reins as Sir Frederick also began to complain. Abruptly, lightning forked down upon them, exploding a large pine tree. Startled, Henry reared up and threw Philippe to the ground and he screamed in agony. Daniel leapt for his friend as Henry began to bolt back the way they came, with Sir Frederick in tow.

Philippe yelled to Daniel over the storm, "Go get, Henry, I'm not going anywhere!"

Five minutes later Daniel returned to the meadow with Henry and Sir Frederick and, luckily, with everything intact. He tied off the animals, knelt to Philippe, and said, "Philippe, are you hurt bad?"

With a look of torture, Philippe groaned, "It appears so, my friend, I landed on this rock on my left side."

Attempting to roll him over, Daniel struggled in agony to help his friend. Philippe's screams were muffled by the wrestling wind and booming thunder. The rain spilled out of the sky in bouncing sheets as Daniel grabbed Philippe with both hands and lifted him onto his back, carrying him to Henry. He managed to get him into the saddle and then they were off, headed to Sacramento and into the storm. The last twenty miles to Sacramento, for Philippe, were the most painful of his entire life. The only way to ride was leaning forward into Henry's mane after throwing back numerous shots of whiskey.

They pulled into Sacramento and found Chang Hui's at dusk, forlorn and exhausted. Chang was nowhere to be seen.

"Philippe, don't move, I will check if he is down the street playing cards," Daniel said.

As he headed for the saloon, Philippe, overwhelmed with pain and fatigue, sat limply on Henry and drifted into a lingering torpor.

Marie met Daniel at the door, her eyes full and eager.

"Hey there, mister, looking for a game?"

"I am looking for Chang Hui, I need his help. My friend, Philippe Galvez, is badly hurt. Is he here?"

She motioned Daniel toward the back of the room.

He entered and said, "Chang Hui, I'm here to ask for your help. My friend, Philippe Galvez, played cards with you several weeks ago, quite terribly I might add, and now he is hurt badly. He was thrown off his horse when it was spooked by lightning, landing hard on his back on a rock."

"Moon Bear, bring me the herbs you collected this morning and I will meet you back at my place," said Chang. Moon Bear left as Chang also got up to leave, collecting his coins.

"Can he walk?" he asked Daniel without looking up.

"He has just ridden over twenty miles to get here, so I doubt it. I left him on his horse."

Galvez lay motionless on Henry, dazed with wrenching pain and whiskey. They slid him onto Daniel's back and went inside the small white door, where the scent of wood smoke lingered in the fading light. Chang lit his lamp and laid him on the bed. His eyes were ripe with glazed agony, and when they removed his pants they found that the entire left side of his lower spine was very swollen and bruised. Chang's fingers lightly danced over Philippe's skin, checking his entire body with methodical precision.

Looking at Daniel, Chang said, "He has fractured vertebrae. The swelling and the bruising, I believe— was caused from him landing on a very important muscle. If so, he has, more than likely, damaged a major nerve, and will have some nerve damage in his left leg."

"What does this muscle do?"

"It connects from your spine to your hips and pelvis. This muscle allows you to walk, basically. We need to turn him over. Galvez, do you understand what I have said?"

"Yes."

"Please, I need you to show me your tongue." Chang demonstrated to Philippe, then asked Moon Bear for his needles. "Before I can help your friend I must clean out his Qi."

"Qi? What is that?"

"Traditional Chinese Medicine enhances healing power and immunity through several means, including herbs, acupuncture, diet, massage, and exercises. We have been practicing it almost three thousand years. Yin and yang are opposing energies in our bodies, such as Earth and Heaven, winter and summer, and happiness and sadness. When yin and yang are in balance, we feel relaxed and powerful. Out of balance, yin and yang can negatively affect your body and your health. There is a life force in all people, known as Qi. Your friend's yin and yang need to be balanced for his body to be healthy; his Qi must be balanced and flowing freely. His Qi is blocked and needs to flow freely. Until this happens, my medicine will not be as effective."

Moon Bear placed a small case on the table and Chang turned to open the case and said, "Let's get some wood on the fire, it needs to be hot in here." As Moon Bear added logs to the fire, Daniel saw an assortment of needles and shorter, very thin cylinders. Chang took the first needle and placed it in a cylinder between Galvez's eyebrows and pushed it into his skin, then a second, and then two in his right ear. Chang then placed needles in Philippe's left hand, between the thumb and wrist, and also at the elbow. Several went in near his spine and each of his big toes. Chang then gave the charge, "Let's move the bed closer to the stove. I need his skin warm."

Moon Bear gently moved the bed as Chang asked, and after placing the teapot on the stove she moved to her herbs and said, "I will make a poultice for his swelling."

48

The next morning Philippe, ragged and fatigued from pain and restless sleep, lay in the darkness of his quarters and pondered his fate. He wondered how long he would be down and worried about the claim.

Daniel entered and said, "I went to the bank and deposited our gold and cash. I'm taking the boat to Isabel's to get our belongings. Chang said that you could be holed up here for a spell, so I will be gone three days and when I return I will head back to our claim. Rest assured, my friend, I will return."

"You are not going to leave me here?"

"I am. Philippe, we can't leave our belongings there forever."

"You are right. I'm not going anywhere. Have a safe and quick journey."

*****

Upon arriving, Daniel stepped off the ferry, saw Isabel's nephew Fernando, and smiled. "Buenos días, Daniel, ¿cómo estás?"

"Buenos días, Fernando. Why are you here?"

"My aunt ordered some supplies, which were to arrive today, but it appears they did not."

"Can I get a ride to Isabel's? I was dreading the walk, to be honest."

"Of course, absolutely, let me tell the ferryman to ask about the supplies and tell him that I will back tomorrow."

As the wagon jaunted up the hill, Fernando asked, "What brings you back to Rancho Monte del Diablo, Senor Benet?"

"Philippe has had a bad accident, his horse got spooked by lightning and threw him and he landed on his back, on a rock. He will be down a while, so I'm here to get our carpetbags and trunk."

Isabel greeted Daniel with warm smile and bronze skin and served a roasted chicken, beans, and beer. They played dominoes and smoked cigars into the evening while Daniel narrated his and Philippe's travels, then poured out his heartache for me.

49

You must do the thing you think you cannot do.

—ELEANOR ROOSEVELT

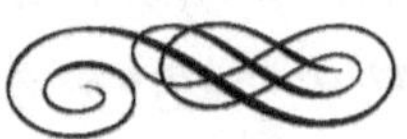

Through my window the day was clear, the palette of a cerulean sky presented itself, luminous and large. I felt a resilience and power that I had not felt since Boston. It was if I was ready to bolt with Bluebell, out of the Carriage House for a tramp in the woods. Neatly folded on the bed of brass were a man's pantaloons, flannel shirt, suspenders, a wool coat, and on the floor in front of them, jackboots. On the bed next to the clothes lay Ashley's Panama hat and his pair of Derringer pistols in a small box of red oak. Without any further doubt or hesitation I stood, my gaze in the mirror reflected back silent and full. I then cast my eyes down to the scissors resting on the Tall Boy dressing table and picked them up without looking. My eyes trance-like and full, I grabbed a handful of my beautiful hair and began to cut it off.

When I was done, I practiced looking like a man in the mirror. After a few moments, I began to laugh deeply, filling in months of despair and sadness with color. Once completely dressed, I decided that I had to feel like a man, to imitate the movements and expressions of a man. I even packed my bag like a man, or so I thought, then as an afterthought I added a tender fusion of coal dust to my face.

I then realized that I had not even thought of what name to use. Sinking back into the Regency rosewood chair, amused, I began make a list of the boys that were in my school classes. As they surfaced from my memory, I listed their names and their attributes:

Albion Thatcher	*smart but arrogant, picked on younger children*
Paris White	*tattletale, played with the girls*
Lofton Quinn	*beat up Farley Hess, a sass-mouth*
Johnson Perry	*polite, thinks quick, always wins*
Farley Hess	*meager in stature and nature*
Ezra Keller	*took piano lessons together—I was better*

My eyes grew large as my body flooded with laughter. "Oh, my, Paris White! Levi's butterfly, the Paper White he called the Paris Virgin, I never put it together, who would have even have thought it. That is so silly." Noticing that I was talking to myself, I paused as the memory of the Paper White butterfly and Daniel Benet tickled at my consciousness.

Albion, Lofton, Johnson, and Ezra all had similar traits, which I attempted to blend into my own man. They were all strong, physically and emotionally, and wanted for the most part be a good person. I imagined that they were all now much better men than they had been boys. I had admired that Ezra had an immense drive to succeed and do his best, even though he could never be the piano player I was. If my chips were going in the wrong direction, I wanted a piece of Ezra with me. Suddenly I glanced back into the mirror, shoulders back, eyes squinting, Ashley's hat riding low on my brow, and in my most convincing man voice I said, "Howdy, name's Ezra Quinn."

50

An idea can turn to dust or magic, depending on the talent that rubs against it.

—BILL BERNBACH

As the newly christened Ezra Quinn stepped onto the boardwalk, into a frenzy of men and animals, I took a ladylike step into the mud and descended the hill to the bay and my awaiting transport to Sacramento. With each step becoming more like Ezra Quinn, and becoming more exhilarated, no one recognized me as a woman. A horse pulling a cart bolted up the hill toward me, plummeting through my thoughts, and I jumped wildly to avoid being trampled. A canteen, thrown from the cart, missed my face by inches.

Once on the bay, for the first time since arriving, I soaked in the enormous, expansive beauty of the bay. The landscape was surreal and profound. The surrounding hills, verdant and inviting after the winter, were stacked at the edge of the unknown. The wind whipped off the crisp, clear water as I and the other travelers sat around the potbellied stoves in the saloon.

Upon arriving in Benicia, I walked to the ferry, which was being loaded with supplies, and nervously asked the ferryman, "Howdy, sir, I'm Ezra Quinn. Do you know a woman named Isabel on the other side of the river?"

"Of course I do, everyone does. Her family has lived here longer than anyone. Why, these are her supplies I am loading right now. She is a good woman."

"Can you take me there?"

The man's face was pruned from the sun, a landscape of ravines scattered randomly and cemented in his history, among a week's growth of stubble. He smiled broadly, revealing broken teeth, and said with mischievously twinkling eyes, "Sonny, I make this trip three times a day. My charge is three dollars. If you have the money, you get the ride."

Once they reached the other side, the ferryman saw Fernando waiting with his wagon.

"You are in luck, partner, Fernando here can take you to Isabel, she is his tía."

"What is a tía?"

"A tía is your aunt, a sister of your mother or father. Son, you're new around here, ain't ya?"

"Yes, actually I'm from San Francisco. I'm trying to meet up with my partners in Sacramento. They are friends of Isabel's."

"Fernando, this here is Mr. Quinn and he is looking for your tía, can you give him a ride?"

"*Si, señor,*" he said, then turning to me. "*Buenos tardes, Señor Quinn. Como estás?*"

"*Bien, gracias, y tu?*" I returned, now feeling quite proud of myself, for at least learning some Spanish while on the *California.*

With the supplies loaded, the two headed up the hill to Isabel's and Fernando asked, "How is it that you know my Tía Isabel?"

"I do not know her, but she has helped my friends, Daniel Benet and Philippe Galvez. I am meeting them in Sacramento."

"You are in luck, Mr. Quinn, Benet is here! He arrived last night. His partner, Philippe, was hurt badly and he has come to pick up their belongings and mail."

The words moved as if in slow motion through my entire body and settled into the abyss of unsettled thoughts. As the wagon crested the hill, I was suspended in a white-hot fear, my mind shuttered with confusion. My whole body trembled as if a New England hurricane was approaching. My upper lip began to perspire. *What would I say to him?* I had not prepared for this. I felt like jumping from the wagon.

Then the feeling suddenly vanished as quick as it appeared. To myself I said, *Damn you, Claire Stewart, confront your fears! This is just another fork in your path. I am either with them or I am still by myself. What I need is a second plan.*

When the wagon reached the house, Fernando yanked the reins hard, and the horses disagreed, smelling fresh hay in the barn. Moments passed as I waited for assistance, forgetting that I was not a woman, but a man. Finally Fernando said, "This is the end of the trail, Mr. Quinn, that is unless you want to help with rubbing down the horses?"

I grabbed my carpetbag, jumped down from the wagon, and walked up the porch steps, stopping at the door, my legs buckling slightly as I walked in. To my surprise, sitting there in the dining room was Daniel, playing dominoes. When I saw him, my bag fell from my hand to the floor, breaching the silence. My knees melted and waned and I felt as though I might faint yet I did not.

My eyes transfixed on Daniel, and the moment stalled uncomfortably until Isabel said, "What can I do for you, young man?"

My eyes shifted from Daniel and then to Isabel and back, as I lifted Ashley's hat and with a weak, apprehensive smile said, "I am Stewart, Claire Stewart."

Daniel sprang from the table toward me, his eyes searching mine as if meeting again for the first time. He held out his hand and said, "I am Benet, Daniel Benet."

I held out my hand with all the dignity and pretense of the lady I wanted to be. Daniel gave my hand a gentle kiss and I felt his mustache. He pulled me into him and held me close, and for the first time, I folded into his frame.

We embraced for what seemed like a moment of forever and then he kissed my neck softly and said, "My God, it is really you, Claire, how are you? I thought I would never see you again. I love you, Claire, I can't deny it any longer."

I held him tightly as my tears of happiness traversed my coal-stained face. In between my sobs I replied, "I'm a mess."

Daniel handed me his handkerchief and said, "The last time I gave you my handkerchief you slapped me so hard the mud flew."

"I was intolerant and smug, you were just trying to be a gentleman."

Isabel stood and began to put away the dominos, not really sure what to make of Daniel holding a woman, dressed in a man's clothes.

Daniel turned me toward her and said, "Isabel, this is Claire, the woman I told you about."

Stepping toward them, she said, "Nice to meet you, Claire. You two, I hear, have had quite the adventure."

"Yes, I suppose it has been."

"Let me take your bag for you, Claire, and I will let you two have some time. Dinner is in about an hour or so."

We walked out under a live oak, which stood massive and regal against a fading blue sky.

As we sat on a log Daniel asked, "Why are you here, Claire?"

"I have been a mess for weeks and weeks and weeks. Ashley's death was a tremendous shock and heartbreak. Even though I am not sure if I really ever loved him or what he was to me. I have acted like such an entitled, spoiled rapscallion. When I read your letter, it was as if floodgates that held back my tremendous sorrow opened, and it was then that I realized that I too felt the same way. I had repressed all of it out of my own sheer stubbornness and now I had neither Ashley nor you. I have been so unkind to you, Daniel, and for that I will forever be sorry."

"Don't be so hard on yourself, Claire. When we met that day in the forest, you were Ashley's girl, and then on the *California* you were his wife. I knew where I stood and I never would have interfered. You have to believe that, Claire."

"I do, Daniel, and I fought to keep you out of my mind. But first I need you to tell me a story."

"What story?"

"Just how did you end up on the *California* in Panama? Were you following me?"

Daniel rolled a soft laugh of endearment, and grabbed my hand, his eyes focused on mine. His expression transformed and he said, "Claire, I did not follow you. I am a gentleman and gentlemen don't chase after another man's wife. I know that you thought I was gawking at you on our journey; I was never aware of that, though Philippe hounded me often. I would never wish to embarrass you or myself with such dishonorable behavior."

I placed my other hand on his and burrowed into his shoulder. Daniel began telling his story of what had happened after he left me in the forest: Mr. Spear and the incredible story of Samuel Fairagain. Upon finishing, he said, "So now I am ready for your story."

Puzzled, I asked, "What story?"

"The story of why in tarnation you are dressed like a man. And what did you do to your beautiful hair?"

******

"Oh, my God, Claire is dressed like a man," shrieked Maeve, bolting Brodie out of a sleepy daze.

"What are you talking about?" Brodie questioned.

"Oh, my God!" Maeve once again declared, her mouth wide.

"What Maeve means Brodie, is that Claire has cut off her hair and is now trying to dress and act like a man."

"Why?" Brodie asked.

Grammy said, "Back then it was not safe for a woman to travel alone."

"Where is she traveling to?"

"She has gone to search for Daniel, sleeping brother!"

"Wow! Did I miss a lot?"

"Duh! They're together now at Isabel's."

Rubbing his eyes, Brodie asked, "How much more to go?"

Smiling, Grammy said, "Almost done, little man."

Grammy's cat Murphy, stretched against the windowsill in his evening slumber as Grammy handed Vanessa the manuscript to read.

51

The pain passes, but the beauty remains.

—Pierre-Auguste Renoir

Philippe's body lay motionless, as his eyes, timid and confused, struggled to focus on the four walls. The white walls before him painted his tapestry of confusion with a sterile calm. Pain radiated through his body, now a burning mélange of lost feelings, with no connections.

Chang handed him a long cylinder of ivory, inlaid with jade, and said, "Here, Philippe, take some puffs of this medicine, it will help with your pain."

After taking several puffs, Philippe felt a strange sensation, totally unlike anything he had ever felt. A gradual numbness crept through his body, his heartbeat now pronounced. The medicine produced a presence of floating from head to foot and a sensation of dreamy exhilaration. It was as if he longed to engage in some active movement, to sing, dance, or leap. After several minutes, the sensation occupied every part of him, and softly lulled him to sleep, numbing his agonizing pain.

He wafted back and forth from dream to reality and when he woke, there was Moon Bear.

"I do not remember the accident, only the result," he said laying upon a sack of bay leaves and herbs, still feeling as if he were dreaming. He continued, crippled by self-pity. "I was told she was not here. Where did she go? Where did my life go?"

"Who is she, Philippe? Your life is right here, you must rest," Moon Bear answered.

"Her name is Gracie, I can't find her."

Drifting away into his dreams, Philippe found himself lying in a hammock beneath a large oak tree, and said to the tree, "Girl, you are one tough rascal, dancing right here in this spot." Her bark was stained by shimmering red lichen, which flanked to the north. His thoughts spiraled as a sweet and tender bird song called to him from the tree. He began to float into the gnarled limbs of the white oak, as the bird song chanted peace, peace. He found himself being pulled by gravity, whirling away from the hammock, searching for the singing bird. But he found no bird, his dream now ice cream melting on a hot day.

He awoke and Chang said, "Time for your lunch, did you have a nice rest? Did you have good dreams?"

Philippe then realized he was back in the blur of the four white walls. His eyes filled with the pain of the universe, he said, "I was listening to the birds and their song was filled with such peace. I was looking for my friend, but I never found her."

Placing his hand on his forehead, Chang said, "I need you to sit up, Philippe. Moon Bear spent the morning collecting herbs for you. She made you some tea of wormwood and Artemisia, along with a poultice of beeswax, wild ginger, mock orange, and pinyon pine. It will help you to heal and will reduce your swelling."

With the slightest movement, Philippe winced and stiffened, but the three of them worked to get him into position. Moon Bear dropped his breeches, revealing his badly swollen and bruised body, and applied the warm poultice and herbs to the injury. She then wrapped his torso in a warm cloth, all while singing a rhythmic chant. When she finished, she walked to the stove and fetched Philippe a cup of tea, and as she set the cup and saucer down, the rattling of warm porcelain sang into the silence. Moon Bear then returned to the stove and lit a bundle of sage. She began to waft the smoke all over Philippe's body while chanting a beautiful song, soaring tender and light while a soothing spring rain drummed on the roof.

<h1 style="text-align:center">52</h1>

The next day, we traveled together to Sacramento, pretending to be brothers, which presented some difficulty.

Daniel was quick to notice that I walked, well, like Claire.

"You don't walk like a man." With their carpetbags loaded onto the wagon and Fernando inside talking to Isabel, he looked at me his face deep and his forehead lined, and said, "You must walk like this."

As he demonstrated, walking toward the wagon, my eyes filled with purpose, centered on him. I attempted to swagger miserably, swaying my hips as I walked one foot in front of the other toward the wagon, in my oversized pantaloons and jackboots.

On our trip upriver, Daniel began his tale of his and Philippe's tramp to the gold fields. I was captured in awe of the story and agreed that gold mining sounded like physically demanding work and prospecting one's claim sounded quite dangerous.

"Tell me more about Philippe, will he be okay? And the Chinaman, what did you say his name was?"

"His name is Chang Hui. He was kidnapped and brought to California about ten years ago. He was a doctor in China, which is why he was kidnapped. His assistant is an orphaned Indian girl who

176

is a medicine woman. She collects herbs and produces salves and various ointments, which they both use. I do not know much about her except that she helped Chang beat Philippe in a card game, then felt sorry for him and let him win the last hand so he won most of his money back. I think she is Chang's good luck charm when he gambles."

"How does she do that?"

"I am not really sure, yet Philippe believes it."

"Does Chang know when Philippe will recover?"

"I am not sure, I hope he will be recovered when we get to Sacramento. He and I were expecting to return to Dry Diggins to get back to our claim. We were not expecting you to join us."

"Daniel, you are taking me with you, right?"

"Claire, it is much too dangerous for you." His face showed his heartfelt concern.

"Daniel, you know me as a woman, yet everyone else sees me as a man."

As we continued traveling upriver, we were absorbed in the imposing landscape, its expanse threaded with the rich greens and browns of feverous spring growth. I then shared my sad story of sinking into a sea of depression after Ashley's death and how I longed for my uncle, Levi, and Bluebell. Daniel said that he too missed his old life and his mother back in Boston. He mentioned the letter he had written to his mother in which he said he missed her corn pone and biscuits and gravy and suggested that more money could be made selling biscuits and cakes then hunting for gold.

At the mention of biscuits and cakes, I became intrigued and coyly asked, "Around here, is baking as dangerous as gold mining? Will they kill you for a tea cake?"

It was as if we had known each other since childhood. As we traveled we talked about everything imaginable, but we kept coming back to biscuits and cakes. By noon, as we ate Isabel's tamales, we began talking of going into the baking business.

I began to name all of my favorites. "Of course all of the men will love each one. We can sell finger biscuits, ladyfingers, chocolate puffs, pound cakes, cupcakes, and carrot cake."

"Slow down there, sugar," he interjected with a widening smile.

"What, you don't like any of those?"

"Yes, Claire, I so long for them, all of them! But perhaps we need to see what we can find, you know, as far as ingredients and such. We are not exactly in downtown Boston. And how will we bake all of these sweet delights?"

"You make a good point. But there are chickens everywhere, so there must be eggs, right? We could buy them from Isabel."

"Now you're talking."

I continued, enthusiasm filling my voice, "Flour should be available, and I've seen plenty of cattle, so there must be milk and butter. Everything is available in San Francisco, for a price."

Interjecting, Daniel said, "The first thing I am going to do is order two thousand bricks, five hundred fire bricks, and a keg of lime."

My nose crinkled, and I responded, "Bricks and lime?"

"For our new oven, sugar!" said Daniel.

"Oh, yes, an oven would be nice," I cooed. "You are so clever, Mr. Daniel Benet."

53

The road of life can only reveal itself as it is traveled,
each turn in the road reveals a surprise. Man's future is hidden.

—ANONYMOUS

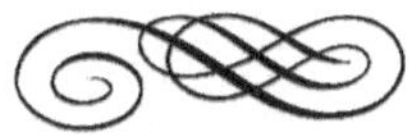

"Philippe, are you awake? It is time for your walk."

Philippe's eyes crawled out of his dream to focus. Moon Bear stood over him in the dark dankness of the room as light from the lone window to the east cast its form on the opposite wall.

"Is there a cup of coffee around, perhaps a biscuit or two?"

"We have tea and rice cake."

"You two are going to turn me into a Chinaman yet."

Moon Bear reached out her arm to grasp him. "No one here is trying to turn you into anything. You are here to heal and now it is time for you to move. Come and grab my arm and we will walk to get you some coffee and a biscuit."

Philippe grabbed her forearm and pulled himself up to her, wincing in pain. He reached to steady himself as a sharp pain radiated through his hip and down his leg, then into his small toe.

"How far are we going, Moon Bear?"

"The biscuits are two doors down from where we went yesterday. When we get back, Chang should be back for your treatment."

As they stepped out onto the boardwalk, the day was warm and soothing and the sky was cloudless.

"Philippe, do not drag your foot, you must pick it up with each step to find your rhythm. If you do not you will lose it forever."

Suddenly three dogs bolted across the street toward Philippe. Moon Bear swung her body to the other side of her patient, and confronted the trio of scallywags as they stopped before her. It was as if they had been transported into obedience.

His eyes stretched wide. "How did you do that? You moved like a cat."

"Do you remember your dreams, Philippe?"

"I do sometimes."

"That is how I do it."

"Do what?"

"I remember my dreams."

Philippe fell silent as he concentrated on lifting his left foot and leg with each small step, as the rhythm of the cane clattered upon the rough boards. A gentle breeze wafted through the grove of ancient sycamores.

The evening before, Philippe and Moon Bear had talked into the night, retelling their stories.

"How did you end up with Sutter?" Philippe asked.

"After my mother and most of my tribe died of malaria in 1833 I was only of two seasons. My father and I wandered the canyons in search of game and collecting food. We had no family or tribe we were a tribe of two. My father was the shaman of our tribe and it was he who was my teacher in the ways of the spirit world. We lived in a remote canyon, on the south slope, in the chaparral, hiding like scared deer from the white trappers. We would still be there today, but after my thirteenth *Kokatim-poko,* summer moon, my father became sick. I suspected malaria, as my medicine did not help him. He became delirious and wandered away from our camp and out of the canyon while I was collecting maidenhair fern and soap root. I tracked him to a large meadow and found him singing to Kakinim, the high spirit guardian. It was there that Sutter's men found us and forced us to work for Sutter."

Now Moon Bear asked, "Philippe, did you love her?"

Philippe finished his step, and as the cane resonated one more clank on the boards he said, "Love whom?"

"Gracie."

A shy, sheepish smile began to fan from the corners of his mouth at the mention of her name. "No, I did not love her, yet perhaps I could have, I suppose. She was strong enough to be my woman."

"But you killed three men for her."

"I killed those men to protect her. They were barbarians! It was the right thing to do. Love had nothing to do with it. She lived two more weeks because of my help."

"So you ran away to California like the other men, for the gold."

"I was not aware that there was gold at the time I was escaping New Orleans. My ride just happened to be a steamer headed for California. And it appears that I am in no shape for gold mining anytime soon. I'll just be happy to be able to ride Henry again."

"Who's Henry?"

"My horse."

Moon Bear pondered the reasoning of the white man giving his animal the name of a man. Then her mind returned to Philippe's plight of not being able to work to support himself and she said, "I know of a place, a spirit place where the sun shines from a pool in the mountains. When you can make the trip, I will take you there during the time of acorns. I have seen us there in my dreams."

"Why go there? For what?"

"There, Philippe, you will discover your purpose."

"What?"

"The path you shall choose in life. There is a stone gift waiting for you."

"A what?"

"*Omeonom yamaniu,* a stone gift for you."

Once back at Chang's, Moon Bear added wood to the stove and put on a pot of water for tea. "Chang should have returned by now. If he is not back when the tea is ready I will see if I can find him."

"I would try the saloon first."

"Chang never gambles without me, Philippe."

Moon Bear poured Daniel's tea and left in search of Chang.

After drinking the tea, Philippe hobbled to his box and found Daniel's pearls. He ran them through his fingers, wondering about their fate. Grasping the hide of the whitetail deer and the map, which depicted parts unknown to him, he began to make a plan for understanding the map and its mystery. Philippe was then interrupted by the appearance of a young boy.

"I don't want my boots shined, boy."

"I am not here to shine your boots, sir. I am here to offer you a proposition."

Philippe was surprised. "Which is?"

The boy raised his hand, which were stubby and caked with living. He had an acorn between his fingers. "I have three cups, and an acorn. I will put it under this cup, and for two bits, I predict that you, in the end, will choose the wrong cup. Game, Mr. Philippe?"

Philippe, intrigued, nodded a yes, and placed a coin on the table alongside the boy's. The cups moved rapidly and in the end Philippe chose, with an exasperated breath, the wrong cup. The boy grabbed the two coins and placed them into his pocket as his brown eyes danced in his unhealthy face.

Just then Daniel sauntered into the room. "Philippe! How are you feeling?"

"Oh, Daniel, you are back! This is my young friend Benjamin and he just wiped me out with his cup trick." With a quick look at his coins, the boy was gone. "Daniel, I fear I may never get back to the claim. I so want to but I can barely walk, let alone ride a horse or do labor. I feel as though I am now a cripple. It will take time."

"Philippe, we are partners, we will be fine."

"What about our claim?"

"Our friends are watching over our claim and they need us to relieve them, to watch over their claims so they can get supplies. Daniel, they are depending on us, they are waiting for us to return."

"Yes, Philippe. But something happened on my trip to Isabel's."

"Which was?"

"It has changed everything."

"What are you talking about?"

"Give me a moment, I will be right back."

Philippe, his face now contorted as his questions stacked like wet lumber, was left waiting for his friend to return. Soon he saw a young man enter the room, with Daniel following.

Daniel's eyes searched his friend for a reaction. "Meet our new partner, Ezra Quinn."

Philippe shot a determined glance at his friend and said, "What are you talking about, a new partner?"

Claire removed Ashley's Panama hat, bowed, face blooming with a smile, and said, "Stewart, Claire Stewart." Then her smile retreated and she said to Daniel, "I don't think he is happy to see me."

"My God, Daniel! How can this be happening? You are in deeper than I thought and now you are dragging me into the whole mess! You said you were going to Isabel's, not San Francisco!"

"Philippe, you must calm down. Please let me explain. I did go to Isabel's. She and I were playing dominoes two nights ago and Claire showed up at Isabel's. You must believe me, I was as shocked as you are." Glancing at Claire, he continued, "I still cannot believe she is here."

Philippe struggled to get to his feet, with Daniel assisting him. "I am happy to see you, Claire, I really am. It is a shock that I could have never foreseen." Reaching out his hands to welcome her, he said, "Welcome to my new prison. It's not the *California,* but I am trapped here just the same."

54

Stop worrying about the potholes in the road and celebrate the journey.

—Barbara Hoffman

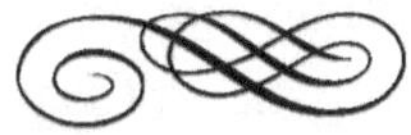

A short time later, Moon Bear arrived, her cheeks flushed and eyes piercing. She brought Chang in tow. Chang, disheveled yet proud as ever, maintained his stoic demeanor. It was clear he was in extreme pain and exhausted.

As the two entered, Philippe declared, "Chang, what has happened? You are injured, please sit here," and he struggled to move for his friend. Chang flopped into a chair as he groaned with a humbled agony.

Moon Bear answered, "He rolled his ankle at the edge of a stream while collecting plants and fell into the ravine. When I found him he was crawling back up to the bank and was almost up to the top. His ankle is swollen but it is not broken, and he may have a cracked rib or two."

Sitting in his chair, his face blotchy and his color waning, Chang said, "Looks like a party in here, Mr. Galvez. You must be feeling better?"

"Yes, a bit, even after I had the shock of my life. This young lad here came in with Daniel, however he is not actually a man, but a woman! Mr. Chang, Moon Bear, let me introduce to you to Claire Stewart," Philippe said, sending a wink in her and Daniel's direction, "who is apparently my new partner."

Moon Bear bowed to Claire graciously. Chang said, "Welcome to our home."

"It is time for your acupuncture treatment," Chang then said to Philippe. "Moon Bear, let's get the fire going and move the bed closer to the stove."

"You must rest your ankle, Chang, acupuncture can wait," Moon Bear instructed.

"I can work sitting down, and I will be done by the time you finish wrapping my ankle," Chang said.

"You are not a very good patient, Chang," Moon Bear replied.

With that Daniel said, "Philippe, Claire and I will go check on the horses. She also needs a horse, and we will get something to eat. Can we bring you back some food?"

Philippe said, "Yes, that would be wonderful," sending Chang and Moon Bear a playful look. "Finally, it will be nice to have some real food for a change."

Moon Bear chided, "You are not starving. You are a fat, lazy coyote."

"Claire and I will be back in a bit, we have a lot to discuss with you."

One by one Chang inserted needles into Philippe as Moon Bear made tea and prepared a salve for Chang's ankle, which was now swollen and discolored.

"You must get off your ankle, you are making it worse."

Sharp ridges fractured the lines of his face. "Yes, Moon Bear, I will. I must finish with Philippe and then I promise I will rest." His tone soft and clear, he said, "I would like for you to bring me a cup of tea," as he inserted another needle.

"I am preparing you a poultice of thistle, snakeroot, and beeswax, the water is heating. Now sit down and get that foot of yours up in the air," commanded Moon Bear.

Philippe interjected, "Chang, it appears that you are now also a patient. I know from firsthand experience that Moon Bear will not put up with any dawdling."

Thirty minutes later, with his foot elevated, Chang removed the last of the needles and settled into a comfortable spot while Philippe dressed with renewed vigor. Grabbing for his cane, Philippe slowly lifted one foot in front of the other as the cane marked the cadence on yellow pine. He went to his box and pulled out two cigars, handing one to Chang as Moon Bear poured the hot water over the herbs.

55

The world belongs to the energetic.

—Ralph Waldo Emerson

After spending a sequestered month together on the *California* without communicating, Daniel and I were making up for lost time. Our conversation easily flowed from subject to subject, as if we were lifelong friends. Several times, while eating dinner at the saloon, we caught ourselves being too close, forgetting my role as a man, which made us chuckle. Almost nine months after our meeting in the forest, we were now becoming comfortable with each other's blue-eyed gaze, slowly sinking into a soothing comfort. Somehow I found myself thinking not of what I had given up, but what I needed to reclaim in my life, this new life in California.

Daniel was apprehensive about telling Philippe of his decision to start a baking business. He was not prepared to lose his friend and business partner over my unexpected arrival.

"Daniel, Philippe is your good friend and business partner. Let us not forget that mining for gold is what both of you chose to do. I do so love the baking business idea, yet let's not pursue any of it until Philippe is ready."

"Thank you, sugar. I just hope that his body will heal and that he can soon walk again."

We agreed that if Philippe wished to continue mining for gold, then that would be what we would do. We found ourselves like magnets, attracted in a pure and wild space, teetering upon the future and standing at the precipice of love. We both were confused by the alchemy of it all.

Philippe, who approached the world logically and practically, weighed his plight after two months with Chang and Moon Bear and realized that baking might suit his new body better than mining gold. Daniel and I worked the claim, with me passing as Philippe's nephew, Ezra Quinn, sharing a tent with four other miners into July. In the span of four weeks, the six of us hauled out forty-two pounds of nuggets. By this time, Philippe was able to walk short distances, with a slight limp and still using a cane.

Daniel and I found a place for our bakery in Dry Diggins. The town was now called Hang Town, after its lawless vigilantes who attempted to enforce some semblance of order by allowing raucous crowds to accuse, convict, and hang the condemned right in the street at the nearest tree. When Philippe was ready to ride a horse, we left Chang and Moon Bear in Sacramento and headed to Hang Town, where the three of us shared a tent as three miners and invested our money into the baking escapade, which we called Hang Town Bakery.

Soon, we were able to purchase ten Dutch ovens. The materials were all delivered and Daniel and Philippe began to construct the ovens. The peel oven was constructed with San Francisco brick—a Roman oven, with thick walls and dampers for greater efficiency. The oven was to be fired in the evening before baking. When the entire oven turned white, including the arch, it was time to remove the fire, which was taken out the oven door and the oven swabbed clean to remove all ashes and dust. Once the hearth was swept and then mopped clean, the damper and door were shut tight, allowing the heat to broadcast over the entire hearth for a period of time. It was not until this process was complete that the oven was ready for baking.

Finally, the ovens were complete and fruit and acorn collecting began. So with that, Daniel, Philippe, and I set out with Moon Bear, with her promise of the Golden Sun Mountain pool, at the time of acorn ripening. Chang, wanting nothing to do with sitting five days on a horse in the stifling September heat, remained in Sacramento.

In the unrelenting heat, we all set out on horseback, and on the third day we came into a huge canyon, which we traveled for two days, until we finally crawled out of the other side of the canyon, reaching the ridge. I had never imagined mountains so high.

Once on the ridge, we came upon a broad plateau sprinkled with a scattering of oaks and conifers, and Moon Bear announced, "We will sleep here tonight and rest, because tomorrow we will be in for some walking."

I wiped the sweat from my forehead. Hot and cranky, I asked, "Why are we even on this jaunt? Can anyone explain that to me?"

"I am taking you to a sacred place of my people. It is a shaman place, the place of your destiny. My people are all gone, so you will now have this place, rather than some ruthless, greedy white man," Moon Bear declared.

While Daniel and Philippe were tending to the horses, two black bear cubs raced into the camp, chomping onto each other's ears and neck, paying no notice to the travelers until Sir Frederick whinnied and spooked the horses. The cubs then noticed them, with obvious shock, and rang out a call for help as Philippe pulled out his rifle from Henry's saddle. The mother of the bear cubs thundered into the camp, mad as hell and up on her haunches. Philippe looked down his rifle barrel at the bear, his finger on the trigger ready to fire. Moon Bear stepped closer to the cubs and their mother and screamed from her depths something bone-chillingly evil, while standing on her toes, arms raised, in imitation of the mother bear's threatening posture. The cubs ran back to their mama, and once the mother bear had her babies with her she moved them back off the plateau, down the slope, and they were gone.

With a gasp of relief, I said, "My God, that was the largest bear I have ever seen." Feeling faint, I moved to a boulder and had a seat.

"We were lucky she was not a grizzly," Moon Bear said.

After our evening meal, Philippe and Daniel settled next to the fire with whiskey and cigars. I too settled my gaze on the fire, which was dancing into the coming darkness, in the time of no moon. Tossing more wood onto the fire, Moon Bear started the Maidu story of how the world began.

She pointed to the west and said, "Out there, where the sun meets the sea and is swallowed, a very long time ago, in the time of the old shaman, the Earth was covered with water, with no land for Coyote on which to walk. Coyote said to the creator, 'In this spot, let us gamble for this world.'"

With a boisterous laugh bouncing off the flames into the new night, Philippe said, "How fitting that Moon Bear's creation story includes gambling." Then he fielded a disdainful look from Moon Bear, and, embarrassed by his insult, Philippe took a slow puff from his cigar.

She continued. "It was the time of salmon and the people had declared a feast. All the while, the Creator tied knots on his counting rope, and during this ancient time he sent his counting ropes to all the people of the Earth. When his ropes were done the Creator needed to speak to his people. He sent runners into the four winds, he sent runners to the sunset and the sunrise. The Creator's message was to come see and to listen to him. After only three days, the leaders of all the people of Earth were there, assembled and hoping to see the Creator and listen to his words."

I jumped as the fire popped suddenly, startling the group as sparks vaulted into the evening sky.

Daniel teased me, his eyes looking up at me from the flames, "Still thinking about that bear?"

Moon Bear continued. "For days the people came, until finally the Creator spoke and told the people, 'Let this world be good, you will have a good world.' Coyote said, 'No! This world will not be good.' This made the Creator very angry, and after much talk Coyote left and the Creator told the people to search carefully around all the borders of the world, even to the edge of the world, where the water meets the land. The Creator told all of the people that Coyote never agreed with him and that he was bad. The people knew that Coyote would lose out, because the people would kill him wherever they saw him.

"So the people walked into the four winds, to the sunset and the sunrise, and all knew Coyote was bad and should be killed. The Creator told the people to look for every place he had peed or shat. 'Look for every place he has scratched the Earth. Listen into the night.' And if they did not hear Coyote after four days, he was dead.

"Coyote walked toward the sunset and lifted his leg into some bushes, then scratched the ground with his hind feet. He went out on to the sandbar on the river and did the same. He jumped into a clump of grass in the river and peed on that. He jumped onto the riverbank and ran away, stopping to pee on every bush he could find and scratching the ground with his hind feet. He did this everywhere he traveled, until he came to the edge of the world, where the sun sets. After some time, Coyote found himself in the middle of the land, and after arriving in the center he found there were no people and the people did not pursue him.

"The five chiefs came together, to track down Coyote, and they ventured out into each of the four winds, looking for places Coyote had pissed and shat and scratched the ground."

Philippe interjected, "This appears to be a double elimination theme here." He gained chuckles from Daniel and me, along with a cold stare from Moon Bear.

"The five chiefs gathered all of Coyote's droppings and brought them all together, and then they captured Coyote and brought him back to the people. They forced Coyote along the riverbank until they reached an island in the middle of the river.

"They told Coyote, 'Here you will die. You think you are so clever and your words so smart. You will starve right here on this island.'

"'Very well,' said Coyote. 'Are you chiefs killing me so you will be great leaders? From every part of this world, you want the people to laugh at me and not you. And you, Creator, everyone will say bad things about you, like that you are not the cleverest.'

"Finally, after Coyote had spoken, he became silent. The others waded across the river onto the riverbank and the Creator said, 'All of you must listen, if you cannot hear Coyote in four days he will be dead.'

"Each night the people listened for Coyote. Coyote sat in silence on the island for a long while then shat. While scratching the ground with his hind feet, he saw a gopher pop his head into the daylight. Coyote said, 'I have a problem, can you help me?'

"Before disappearing into the hole the gopher said, 'If you stay here, you will die.' A bunch of grass appeared in the hole and Coyote asked, 'How shall I survive, please tell me your advice.'

'You must turn yourself into the mist that lingers over the water, as the day heats, the mist will rise you across the river. When you reach the other side, you must call out, and all of your places, where you pissed and shat and scratched—even into the high country where you have pissed on a bunch of grass—these places are yours and will call you.'

"As the beginning of day pronounced the first light, the mist lingered over the river and Coyote danced into the mist as it floated him away from the island in silence. As he landed on the riverbank he sunk his hind claws into the sand and called out. In the far distance he heard an answer, and it was from all of his places where he had pissed and shat and from the places where he scratched with his hind claws.

"The people heard Coyote's call and everyone knew he was alive. All of the people in the world talked amongst themselves and chanted, 'He did not die, he did not die.' Because of this, the people thought that they might also die themselves."

I interrupted, saying, "Goodness, gracious, that is a sad, sad story."

Moon Bear's eyes tracked though the flames and continued. "'You must track him down,' cried the Creator. 'Chiefs, all of you call out to your people, you must find him. Go to the four winds, go to the sunrise, go to the sunset. Let his path warm you to his trail.' The Creator was forceful. 'You must track him down. You must not lose him.'

"After many moons, the people caught up with Coyote and presented him with all that he had pissed and shat and scratched with his hind legs. Everything Coyote had done, they brought it all together into a pile and placed Coyote in the middle of it and watered it.

"After a short time a tree grew, large and stout, with Coyote trapped inside." The people said, 'This is the end of you and all of your trouble Coyote! After four mornings and you do not call out, you will be dead!' "The people went off in every direction and listened to the land."

"A pileated woodpecker flew to the tree and began tapping the tree with its beak. *Tap, tap, tap,* the woodpecker worked meticulously until the sun sank into the sea. The next morning, the woodpecker returned to the tree and continued to *tap, tap, tap* on the tree in the same spot, and finally the hole broke through the hollow trunk.

"Coyote saw Woodpecker poking his body into the tree and said, 'Cousin, would it be possible for you to make the hole just a little larger, for me to pass?' Having made his mark on the hollow tree, the woodpecker flew off, not to return. Coyote then began to feel remorseful about his behavior and spoke out that he had not been good and what he had done was bad. After a short time, a gopher's head appeared, and Coyote said, 'Please help me, what am I to do? Speak to me and do not lie.'

"'There is nothing for you to do. You are to stay here forever and die.'

"'You have never spoken well of me, you never help,' Coyote complained.

"Then another gopher head came out. 'What shall I do?' said Coyote. 'Please speak to me.'

"'There is only one thing for you to do and that is to make yourself into a fog and pass yourself through the hole.'

"On the fourth morning, as the dawn unfolded, Coyote passed completely through the hole and scratched his hind legs and howled out into the land. All of where he had traveled called back to him.

"The next morning the Creator called all the chiefs and declared, 'Rain and snow will always be in the world, and the water will rise and the land will flood. The people must build a canoe to float in the rising water. As the water rises over each mountain, Coyote will be destroyed and only the people will survive.' The people worked hard on the canoe and didn't know that Coyote had changed into a human and worked, laughed, and played amongst the people.

"Finally, after several winters of rain and snow all of the mountains of the world were flooded with water. The people drifted in their canoes until they found land, and suddenly Coyote jumped onto the land and declared, 'I touched the land first.'

"The Creator, who had been next to Coyote the entire time, was in disbelief and said finally, 'Coyote you have much power, I have long tried to kill you and I cannot.' Coyote was now tramping along the ridge. The creator called to him and said, 'Coyote, travel anywhere you wish. The people will not bother you.'

"That was the day Coyote began searching for his wife."

I asked, "What is the meaning of all of the pissing and shitting? The message of the story seems to be to spread it around, as to not foul the world with it."

"We all have our place in the world. Coyote feels that it is important to define his place. The Earth is a place that is neither all good nor all bad. It can be a place of treachery and death, but there are times of great joy and also great pain. There will always be happiness and sadness, laughter and anger. Everyone will die someday. We all have a chance to walk the Earth. The story is not just about the creation of our world, because it determines how our world will be and continue to be forever."

Daniel asked, "What happened next, Moon Bear?"

"Coyote searched for a wife, but that is a different story. It is late and we have a big day tomorrow."

"I think Coyote will find more than one wife," Philippe said with a smile, as he tossed his cigar into the fire.

56

We can never get enough of what we don't really need.

—MATTHEW KELLY

At first light I was entranced in a dreamy slumber. I was with Daniel and Philippe in a driving rain with a strong wind. We were walking on a trail, struggling, and I turned to speak with Philippe. In the distance, carried by the drifting wind, I heard the faint call of a Stellars Jay, *shack-sheck-sheck-sheck.* Suddenly I saw Daniel begin to fall, then the jay squawked loudly, overtaking the sound of the wind and the rain with his harsh nasal alarm, *wah-wah-wah-wah.* My eyes opened to the new day and began to focus on a big blue sky. Above me, a Stellars jay squawked, *shack-sheck-sheck-sheck,* and flew off, dislodging a piece of bark, which floated downward, just missing my face. The moment dangled, but the dream slowly evaporated, and I lay silent with sleep lingering in my subconscious.

"What's happening with those cakes you said that you were going to make, sugar?" Daniel asked.

My cheese biscuits with Moon Bear's herbs were already popular with the miners. Daniel and Philippe had pleaded with me to focus on just three recipes, yet I persisted in creating five. They both were spoiled by my johnnycakes.

Philippe said, "Daniel, let her at least get out of bed first."

"Philippe, he is a man, and that is what men do," Moon Bear said, coming in with an armload of wood.

Now looking at Philippe, then Daniel, Moon Bear dropped the wood she had collected and with a coy smile, and said, "Daniel has the manners of an old dog riddled with fleas."

Philippe roared at Moon Bear's teasing. I was humored by the banter, as I ventured into the brush to do my morning business. I thought, *Ashley would have said the exact same thing. What's happening with those cakes you said that you were going to make, sugar?* Suddenly I saw the two men as quite similar, in a way I hadn't yet realized, which left a slow burn of contemplation.

By the time I returned, Daniel had brought out my Dutch oven and all of my ingredients, and organized them neatly on a flat boulder. "Why, Daniel, you have everything ready, you are so much my huckleberry." At the sound of my words, I realized I sounded as if I was talking to Ashley, and suddenly I began to question who I really was. An odd sensation trickled slowly over the surface of my skin and left my thoughts tangling on the precipice of something I could not explain.

An hour later, Moon Bear stood pointing into the canyon, showing us the direction we would take. I asked, "Why did we climb all the way up here just to go back down the other side? Couldn't we have just gone up this canyon, instead of the one we did?"

"It is impossible to reach the pool from this canyon. We must drop down into the sacred pool from here. It is the only way."

With that, we were off, headed down the other side of the mesa. The day before, we had ridden in the shade of the forest. Now, on the south-facing slope, we began traversing through thick chaparral under the blistering sun now upon us.

"We are now entering the sacred land of my people. Maidu shamans have been collecting herbs in this canyon since the beginning of our people. It is here, with my father, that I saw my calling for my people. Yet now my people are no more. They are dead or scattered to the winds.

"I am a tribe of one."

After a long silence, Moon Bear began to name all the plants and how they were used. We three were silently lulled by the gentle rhythm of our saddles while Moon Bear collected samples of plants that she could reach. We began to hear the faintly muffled sounds of quail and water drifting upward and out of the canyon.

Upon entering a grove of canyon oaks, Moon Bear declared, "To get to the pool we must leave the horses here. There is good bunch grass for them and afternoon shade. We must walk in from this grove and then back out, and we will camp here tonight." From the looks of it the grove had been a camp for a very long time. A large outcrop of boulders faced the east, adorned with petroglyphs that held the ancient story of the Maidu. Moon Bear described each story in animated detail.

"It is here where Kakinim, the high spirit guardian, dwells. Tonight, we shall awaken him and ask for his blessing. I must prepare. I will return just after sunset."

Shortly after sunset, without sound or warning, Moon Bear appeared, startling me as she screamed into the coming darkness. She approached the dancing light of the fire, her body painted a ghost white with overlapping lines of nutmeg charcoal. She wore a summer apron of maple bark fore and aft, with strips of buckskin decorated with deer hooves, pine nuts, and abalone. Clamshell disk beads weighted heavy on her neck. Her presence was illuminated by the reflection of the growing fire. Her earplugs of pelican bone glistened against the light of the fire. She wore a flat top summer hat of woven hazel shoots, bear grass, maidenhair fern, and feathers of the yellow hammer and falcon, all in a full and twisted overlay of shells. She wore summer moccasins and leggings of deer hide. In her hands she carried a cocoon rattle and a split elder baton painted white.

After several moments, Moon Bear began chanting in her methodical drone and swayed in an ancient rhythm. The clapper rattle and baton resonated in her hands, through the fire and into the canyon. She danced into the fire while holding a smoldering bundle of white sage and began to smudge the group. From under her apron she presented a long root of angelica, oozing a bright green slime to the heavens, and she placed it strategically in the coals. With arms outstretched like an eagle in flight, she fanned the flames as smoke dove to the ground like a creeping tule fog. We sat mesmerized by the swaying rhythms of Moon Bear's cocoon rattle and baton, as the smoke crawled toward us.

Daniel's eyes dreaming, his face contoured by the moment, he said, "Coyote."

Moon Bear chanted and sang to her spirit world, while the fire-light danced with the shadows and petroglyphs. The three of us eventually fell into a deep, dreaming sleep as Moon Bear danced into the night.

57

Earth provides enough to satisfy every man's need
but not every man's greed.

—MAHATMA GANDHI

The next morning, smoke wafted upward toward the south from spent embers of canyon oak. I stoked them with manzanita and began to prepare some johnnycakes, bacon, and coffee. Philippe, still having trouble moving in the morning, struggled up off the ground as several young male crows cawed into the morning.

While Daniel tended to the horses, Moon Bear suddenly appeared, hair wet from bathing in the river. She had collected a bundle of tobacco and said, "We must leave soon there is much to do. The horses have to be watered and left with grass because we will not return until afternoon."

Philippe said, "Daniel, let's take the horses down to the river for some water—and don't let me forget the rope, we may need it. Moon Bear said the trail is steep and narrow. Let's collect some grass too, and when we get back our breakfast should be ready."

As the men left for the water, I said to Moon Bear, "What was that you were doing last night? It was beautiful."

"I was calling up Kakinim, asking for his help and blessing, and for your dreams."

"My dreams? I don't understand."

"I placed angelica root into the fire, do you remember what happened?" asked Moon Bear.

I reached into my memory and Moon Bear continued, "The smoke, do you remember what the smoke did?"

"Yes, it crawled along the ground. It was the oddest thing."

"Do you remember your dreams, Claire?"

"From last night? I was in this beautiful place, with many flowers and water flowing. A butterfly, a hummingbird, and a dragonfly followed me everywhere I went. They were swimming in the air around my head and it felt"—I searched for the words—"warm and peaceful."

"This spot, my people have used for thousands of moons, it is our place of power," said Moon Bear. "It is here, the entrance to the portal of the ancient ones, we are at the sacred entrance to the other side."

"The other side of what?"

"The dream world, our spirit world, home to those that wish to help us and protect us, bring us luck—yet also home to those who prey on us. They lurk in the darkness, wishing our misfortune. It is the way of the world."

"I don't understand, Moon Bear, how does this happen?"

"In your dreams, Claire, you saw a butterfly, a hummingbird, and a dragonfly."

"Yes."

"Most people are lucky to see only one animal and you saw three! These animals from your dreams, they have great power, they will protect you forever. It is a very good sign. They are forever your guardians, your spirit guides in this world. You must learn to speak to them, they will listen."

As Moon Bear began to leave to collect grass for the horses, I said, "Moon Bear, are you still not eating today?"

"No, I am not, thank you."

As I laid down the first johnnycake and it slowly began to simmer in the pan, my mind drifted back to the conversation, as if to sort out its meaning. Flipping the johnnycakes, now dancing in the skillet, I moved the pan onto some slow-burning coals at the side of the fire, wondering what the other three had dreamed.

By the time we left camp, the day was warm and oddly humid. We followed the trail into the canyon along the rocky slope of manzanita and mountain mahogany, then into the shade of oaks, conifers, and alder to the south, following a small river, as the sound of falling water grew louder. Moon Bear took her time collecting golden-back and maidenhair ferns and soap root, while chanting rhythmically along the shaded footpath. A fallen log stretched across the swift water.

Seeing that Moon Bear was headed toward the log, which was stretched across the ravine five feet above the water, I stopped, my hands now on my hips, and announced, "I am not going to walk across that! I will not do that! I will fall."

Ignoring me, Moon Bear led the way on nimble feet. A moment later she was on the other side.

Daniel attempted to coax me, "Claire, I will help you, I will be right behind you, holding you so you feel steady. You can do this."

"Yes, Claire." Moon Bear now walked back on the log toward her, reaching out her hand.

"Take my hand, we will do this together."

Perspiration spread like a coming tide on my upper lip. My mind flashed back to Garland falling into the ice as if in slow motion. The rushing water below grew louder. Focused on Moon Bear, I reached out my hand, which trembled. From behind, Daniel steadied my forward movement as I inched slowly across the log. Philippe then crossed with a measured caution, his own fall from Henry fresh in his memory.

Once safely across, we walked to a rock ledge. Below us, the forest opened into a large circle and the pool, clear and inviting, came into view. Moon Bear declared, "We are here! Golden Sun Mountain Pool." Philippe and Daniel were amazed at the amount of water flowing, despite how late in the dry season it was—below we could see a series of falls that dropped out of each pool, one after the other, with water rushing into the canyon below.

"What is that in the pool?" I asked.

"It is the sun from the other side, the dream world," Moon Bear explained.

Daniel and Philippe glanced at each other, both thinking the same thing, questioning the logic of what Moon Bear had said. I could see that both of them were contemplating the reality of Moon Bear's words, as a distinct coldness traveled the length of my spine.

Moon Bear continued by describing the path that we would need to take, a zigzag down the opposite side of the pool, covered with several types of ferns and stone crops, finally arriving at the lower falls.

Moon Bear presented an astute calmness as she continued her low chanting for several moments. Then she said, "*Omeonom yamaniu,* stone gift for you." Her eyes tracked Daniel and Philippe and said, "Both of you have dreamed of the stone, it is your destiny." They followed a narrow, shaded path, wet and lush with growth, to the pool. Once at the edge of the pool, Daniel and Philippe looked up, awed with the falls' beauty. As her father had to her, Moon Bear instructed Philippe and Daniel to dive into the pool and swim into the swirling water and grab a charm.

Daniel said, "I think that that is not the sun but gold."

"I think so, too," repeated Philippe.

"Claire, Moon Bear, pardon us while we get into our short drawers. Could you please turn away?"

We turned our heads to the ridge behind them, and watched the dark clouds that began to gather up the slope, signaling a coming storm. Thunder rumbled softly in the far distance. Looking to the clouds coming in swiftly from the south, Moon Bear said, "*Weh-tehm-teh-mi: thunderstorm.*"

Philippe found the water the coldest he had ever felt, having grown up in Louisiana, but after the initial shock he appeared surprised by how easily his body moved in the water. With a renewed vigor, he swooped his arms and kicked downward, toward the golden light, and at ten feet, out of breath, he returned to the surface, breathing deep and large. Daniel, with quick strokes, dove, reaching for the light, as bubbles rose, clouding his vision. He touched not the sun, but a boulder of gold, and the last bit of air seemed to scream from his lungs as he pushed to the surface. Philippe dove down through the bubbles and attempted to grab the boulder, which was circular, about four inches thick and over two feet around, molded over the boulder it sat upon. He was surprised by its weight and left it where it sat, returning to the surface.

Gathering his breath, he said to Daniel, gasping for air, "It is too heavy to bring it up. I think we should use the rope."

"Fishing is good," Moon Bear added.

I sat there confused by her words, then laughed, realizing her metaphor.

"I want to try one more time," Daniel said.

"Sure, tell me if you think the water is warmer near the bottom, it seemed warmer to me," Philippe said.

Looking at me, Moon Bear said, "*Polpolpolim*, hot water bubbling."

With one last breath, Daniel was gone, but in a few moments he was back on the surface. "You're right, we need the rope, and yes, the water is warmer."

I got up from the boulder I was sitting on and passed the rope to Daniel, who said, "Hold on to the other end," as he began to make a loop to cradle the boulder. Moon Bear sat silently, trance-like, as the Earth began a soft, rolling shake.

My eyes searched Moon Bear's face, wide and fearful. "What is happening?"

As several small rocks began to fall from above, Moon Bear said, "*Yswalulum,* Devil Coyote."

"Earthquake," Philippe announced. "I studied a bit of geology at the university in Baton Rouge."

"You went to a university?" My head leaned to the side, pondering this new information.

"Yes, my mother said it was one of my father's last wishes, so I went for a few years, then I tired eventually with all of the pretentious pomp of it all," Philippe said.

I found it odd that I had never considered Philippe or Daniel having been to college. I wondered what else I had missed about them both.

"Philippe, what do you think?" Daniel said, showing him the knotted rope.

"Looks good, my friend," Philippe said.

With a deep breath Daniel dove through the bubbles and began to place the rope under the boulder. His lungs empty, he returned to the surface.

Facing the trio from the middle of the pool, while gasping deep breaths, he said, "Almost there," and disappeared again under the water.

"Wait, let me help," Philippe shouted over the falling water.

"He has chosen his path," Moon Bear declared.

Daniel dove back into the warm, swirling bubbles and began to place the boulder into his rope sling. Finally, having secured the boulder and the sling, he thrust through the water to the surface, gasping for breath. "It's done, reel it in."

With a wide grin Philippe said, "My friend, you hooked the big fish, you should be the one to haul it out."

I mooned, and said with a curtsy, "My hero!"

Philippe jumped onto a large boulder as Daniel, filled with pride, took the rope and began to slowly dislodge the boulder out of its ancestral home. Philippe helped guide the way.

Daniel said, "Feels about thirty-five pounds," and they both brought it out of the water. A ripple of excitement stirred in Golden Sun Mountain Pool.

Moon Bear broke the moment, saying, "Come winter, you both shall catch many salmon."

"Yes, we will, Moon Bear, all of us together." Philippe answered.

Worried about Philippe's physical condition, Daniel demanded to carry the boulder. He walked out of the pool, and up and out along the narrow path, while a light rain drizzled over polyploidies, green like velvet, and a darkening backdrop of clouds moved in.

Philippe asked Moon Bear, "What did you call this?"

"*Omeonom Yamaniu,* Stone Gift."

Daniel beamed, "This is an amazing find, Moon Bear. This is worth thousands of dollars."

58

*Ever has it been that love knows not its own depth
until the hour of separation.*

—Kahlil Gibran

As Philippe and Daniel got dressed, Moon Bear, in a chanting trance, slumbered up the narrow path, away from the pool, not hearing the thunder rumbling in the distance. When we entered the grove where conifers, oaks, and alders danced in the wind, a group of young male crows cawed a persistent chorus.

An icy rash spread over my skin and the sound of the rushing water overtook my thoughts and reverberated in the forest, mottled and yet somehow clear. Now at the log, I spotted a dragonfly skimming the air around my head, which somehow gave me courage. I thought to myself: *what goes in must come out.*

Moon Bear crossed first and then helped me. I felt proud of my newfound courage, as I arrived at the other side of the river. Philippe crossed next, as thunder again rumbled, louder and closer. Carrying the Stone Gift, Daniel began to cross the log. A young crow up in the canopy of trees squawked loudly and flew off over the rushing water. As Daniel inched across the log, the Earth suddenly shook hard with a swift jolt. The log shifted with the shaking and broke in two. As Daniel fell, he heaved the gold toward the group and fell into the churning water, his head striking a boulder. My and Philippe's terrified screams resonated long and deep into the canyon, as Daniel's body swiftly went over the falls and disappeared. We raced down the path as the rain began to fall.

My wailing continued, my agony painfully cascading into the canyon. My entire body shook from shock, and I replayed what I had seen: the gift landing on the bank, and Daniel's body careening over the falls. A chorus clamored from the trees above as large drops of rain began to fall. My whole body trembled in white-hot fear, the weight of the shock compressing my senses. Philippe and I ran to Daniel, and we found him lying facedown in the middle of the pool, the water stained red, its color meandering over the lower falls.

Philippe retrieved Daniel's lifeless body, and Moon Bear went up the path to bring his horse down to the stream. Philippe carried Daniel to the horse on his back, his body shaking in agony. We walked out of the canyon, shocked into silence.

****

Vanessa inhaled a solemn breath filled with sadness. Watching the children and Grammy sleeping, she sat in silence while Murphy's soft purr filled the room. *Poor Claire,* she thought. *So much death surrounded her life. How will she cope?*

And at this moment, she resolved the fact that she, like Claire, also had death surrounding her. She pondered what her therapist had shared years earlier. *Vanessa, in our lives, even though we wish to control things that happen, there really are very few things we can control, and death is not one of them.*

Remembering what Grammy had said earlier, "and the plot thickens," Vanessa continued to read.

59

Challenges in life can either enrich you or poison you.
You are the one who decides.

—STEVE MARABOLI

I sat on the bluff, my entire essence flooded with confusion, my sorrow tumbling aimlessly, like the river below. *Why did he have to die? Why is this godforsaken death hovering over me, lurking in the shadows?* It was as if summer had inhaled its last breath and held it for too long, fracturing all in its path. I was like an egg broken, my life fluid flowing sticky and viscous over the landscape, beginning to curdle in the afternoon heat.

The hot breath of the storm blew through the trees as leaves danced in the wind, and Philippe and Moon Bear began to untie Daniel from Buttons.

"What are you doing?" I asked them in alarm. My eyes flooded with tears, I faced Moon Bear and screamed, "Why did you bring us here?"

"For you to find your purpose."

"Find my purpose—what, for Daniel to die?"

"Daniel chose his own path and now here we are on ours."

"He needs to be buried, Claire," said Philippe.

"Bury him here? And have some animal dig him up and scatter him all over the canyon?" I continued, my face smudged with dirt and tears. "He deserves better and you know it, Philippe. Leave him on the horse, we're taking him to Hang Town for a proper burial."

"He will lose his spirit, and if that happens he will lose his way," Moon Bear flatly declared. "My people bury after a night of wailing."

"I want to visit him in Hang Town."

"Then he will lose his soul and his way, leaving him trapped between both worlds. His body will swell soon."

Philippe pleaded, "It could be over three days before we get back and he will be decomposing the whole way."

I sat down on a boulder and again began to cry. A memory of my childhood came to me suddenly, of a dead cow I once saw in the far meadow. I was ten years old and came upon it while riding my pony. It was the rotting stench I noticed first, then the bloating. It had swollen immensely, as if ready to explode in every direction. Levi had said she had been dead about three days. Abruptly, the thought of that happening to Daniel turned my whole system inside out and I vomited.

Moon Bear and Philippe rushed to my side and I said, looking to the west, the sun dancing on leaves, wet from the afternoon storm, "Daniel was not an animal. He must be buried with dignity."

A sheltered hum of silence came over us. Then Moon Bear began a song of mourning, as the storm retreated up the slope above us. Moon Bear surveyed the bluff as her rhythmic chant floated lightly on the wind. When she returned, she measured Daniel with the rope, from his head to his groin. She and Philippe used that distance to draw a circle, then the three of us walked back down into the canyon to collect digging sticks of mountain mahogany.

We dug all the next day, and finally had a circular grave over six feet in diameter and three feet deep. Moon Bear collected some sacred burial plants and assured us that the moon would watch over his spirit and every acorn moon would shine on him.

Moon Bear collected a handful of white sage, tying it into a tight cylinder with stems of maidenhair fern. She lit the bundle and the pungent smoke wafted on a gentle breeze while bushtits and quail sang from the underbrush. She drew the smoke to the four corners of the grave, singing prayers for Daniel. She handed me the bundle as she and Philippe placed Daniel into his final resting place. Taking the sage from me, with three quick breaths, she revived the smoldering herb, then blew the smoke from Daniel's head down to his toes and to each side, her song dancing into the sky as the smoke rolled gently over Daniel's still body. Philippe and I, with hastily chosen words, prayed for his soul. I felt my pain wailing, and I knew I would carry it to my own grave. We collected rocks, as big as we could lift, to fill in the surface of the circle, to discourage animals from digging.

60

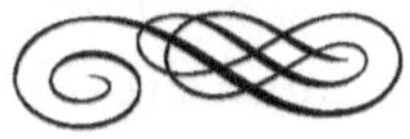

October 6, 1849

Dearest Uncle,

My heart and spirit have been wounded again by death. My friend Daniel Benet had a terrible accident and is now dead. He and his friend Philippe traveled with Ashley and me on the *California*. They both gave me comfort and support after Ashley's passing, and now Daniel is gone too. My heart is left with the horrific scar of their deaths. Why is it that so many have died around me? My parents, my aunt, Garland, my husband, and now Daniel. I feel as though my life is evaporating like a waning tide, pulling me into the shallows. Why is it that each time I become truly happy, fate grabs hold of me and shakes the joy right out of my heart?

Philippe and I, determined to work through the loss of our friend, have continued with the bakery the three of us had started. The bakery was Daniel's idea, and it is making quite a bit of revenue. It is also too much work for just the two of us. We are working over sixteen hours a day, sleeping in shifts. We have hired two married women to help with the baking. By noon each day we are all sold out of everything, as our supply cannot meet the demand.

Philippe is quite the wood worker. He has built a countertop the full length of the shop, and shelves to display our breads and cakes. We have ordered lamps, which should arrive in three weeks or so. So the bakery business is doing much better than either of us ever dreamed. It has kept us busy.

Occasionally my mind drifts back to Ashley and our short time together. I have realized that I never really loved Ashley. I only loved the thought of loving him. I have come to accept that it was Daniel whom I loved, not Ashley. It was love at first sight. We both felt it, struggled with it and fought off our feelings for months. Even when we both found ourselves trapped on the *California,* with me married to Ashley, we continued to deny our feelings. When I found him again, it was a truly special day. We both felt like we had known each other since childhood.

Philippe was like a brother to Daniel, and we're both devastated by his death. Philippe is my friend and business partner, my protector and confidant. I have sent for my ship captain's box and the rest of my belongings, which I left behind in San Francisco. I long for a new piano to play. I plan on making a stand here with our bakery in Dry Diggins, which is now being called Hang Town due to the gangs of vigilantes who hold court in the streets and hang those they deem guilty on the nearest tree. It is a wild and lawless place, teetering upon the precipice of civilization.

Philippe and Daniel met a man employed with the Pacific Mail Steamship Company while they were traveling together. His name was James Kent and he died on the journey across the isthmus. He asked Philippe and Daniel to find some gold nuggets and send one to his wife. We have found many gold nuggets. We found a thirty-eight-pound boulder of solid gold! Daniel was carrying it when he died. I am hoping that you can find Mrs. Kent and tell her about her husband's passing and give her this nugget for us.

I imagine that you are preparing for the beautiful New England winter, which for some wild reason, I miss terribly. Please give my best to Levi.

I love you,

Claire

61

Vanessa closed the book and said, "Daniel is dead I can't believe it." She looked at her children and grandmother, all still sleeping, and realized it was late in the evening. She took a long breath and her thoughts drifted back to the circle of death in Claire's life and her own. Much like Claire, Vanessa had discovered that life always moved forward, regardless of the good or bad. She woke the children and told them it was time for bed.

"What about the story?" Brodie complained sleepily, rubbing his eyes.

"I fell asleep, Mom, what did I miss?" Maeve asked.

"We'll finish it in the morning, sweetie."

After putting the children to bed, she leaned in to wake her Grammy and noticed her skin was quite pale and cool to the touch. Suddenly Vanessa's own body was flushed and hot, her fingers trembled. "Grammy, it is time for bed, let's get up," Vanessa said, as she shook her lightly. When she reached to feel her pulse, Vanessa's greatest fear was realized. She pushed the call button on her Grammy's wrist, and moments later Leah arrived and confirmed her fears.

"I am so sorry, Vanessa. But she is now in a restful place. I will make some calls and have someone come out here to help us."

Every single memory of her Grammy seemed to well up at once and her tears began to flood. All of these years, wrapped inside her loss, it had never occurred to her that her Grammy had her own pain to bear. But she had discovered, today, a side of her Grammy she had never noticed, her playful, loving side and for that, she felt blessed. She thought: *How did I miss that for so long? Was I really that absorbed in my own story?*

Around midnight, the paramedics finally left with Grammy, and as they drove out down the hill, Vanessa stared into the taillights.

"Goodbye, Grammy, thank you for loving me and my children." Her tears welled up again and she said, "We love you Grammy, we will love you always."

Vanessa went upstairs and watched Maeve and Brodie sleep for a while. "Never forget the joy and wonder of your childhood," she said to them as tears crawled across her cheeks, and then she crawled under the covers with her children and fell asleep.

She found herself floating on her back in a pool at the base of a waterfall, her hair splayed out in every direction. The tumbling water above her became lighter and lighter, and she found herself awakened out of her dream by Brodie's voice.

"Come on, Maeve, let's find Grammy, we need to finish the rest of the story."

When Vanessa opened her eyes they were gone. She called out, "Maeve, Brodie, come back, I have something to tell you." Their feet padded over the ancient fir floor, and they made their way back to their mother.

Vanessa took in a deep breath, then released a prayer and said, "Come sit with me."

The children hopped back up on the bed and happily folded into their mother, embraced by her soothing and familiar smell.

"Last night you both fell sleep, and Grammy too, so I stopped reading and put you both to bed. I went back to the parlor to wake up Grammy and she wouldn't wake up."

"Why not, Mom?" Brodie questioned.

Maeve brought her hands to her mouth and said, "Oh, no!"

"Our Grammy," Vanessa said as her tears began to well up, "passed away last night while I was reading the story."

The children started to cry too, and the three of them cuddled under the covers and had a good cry together.

Brodie asked, "Can we see her?"

"They came and got her last night, they left around midnight."

"Why?" Maeve and Brodie both wanted to know.

"Grammy had what is called an advance health care directive."

"What's that?" They both asked.

"It directs people on what to do when you die."

Brodie asked, "You can do that?"

"Yes, you can, and Grammy said in her directive that if she passed, she wanted to be taken away as soon as possible, so that is what happened. That's what she wanted."

"Why did she have to die?" Brodie pouted.

"She lived a long and fanciful life and was able to experience many wonderful things. When I was little, she would drag me to see the Vienna Boys Choir or to see some fancy European dressage horses, and I thought at the time that it was so awfully boring. But as I think about it now, it was all so fascinating. We will remember her forever and that is special."

"She was the most special Grammy ever," Brodie said, as tears overtook him once again.

62

The more decisions that you are forced to make alone,
the more you are aware of your freedom to choose.

—THORNTON WILDER

Leah made a breakfast of poached eggs, bacon, and hash browns. While serving them, she said, "Your Grammy had requested this breakfast yesterday for all of you, she even requested that I put vinegar in the water for the poached eggs."

Vanessa said, "She lived her life on her terms."

"Yes, she did. I wish that I had known her better. I found this letter that she left for you on her desk."

As the children were packing their things, Vanessa sat in the porch swing that she and Emily had played for hours in as children. Her memories, grounded to this place, this family place, surrounded her. She gazed at the river for a long moment as an Anna's hummingbird scouted the trumpet vine blooming on the veranda. Holding the envelope in her hands, she said to the hummingbird, "Goodbye, Grammy, I love you." Her vision blurring from her tears, Vanessa opened the envelope and began to read.

March 11, 1997

My Dearest Vanessa,

If you are reading this, I am in another place. No worries, I am fine. I want you to know that I love you, Vanessa, and your chickabiddies, so terribly much. I am writing this to you because I know my fate awaits me with every one of my breaths, I feel it deep inside waiting.

There is a ship captain's box in a hidden passageway in my home and it holds the story of my great Grammy Claire. This box traveled to California with her at the beginning of the gold rush and holds her story about traveling in a steamship around Cape Horn to California and the many challenges she faced once arriving in San Francisco. In case something happened to me before your visit, I didn't want to leave you and your children without her story. Like Maeve, I wanted to interview my Great-Grammy Claire. At the time, she had not finished her story. She promised me she would finish her story someday. Unfortunately, she died before finishing it. I learned that she and my great-grandfather were true adventurers and they had a passion for adventure, discovery, love, and family.

The last challenge of the box took me years to discover. There are six secret compartments in the box, where you will find Great-Grammy Claire's story of the man she loved and lost, along with her most prized possessions. I had hoped for years to add the last pages she wrote to her book, but then I could not physically get to the box. Sometimes life just gets in the way and sometimes life just walks out the door.

Vanessa, I am so very sorry about the way I have acted toward you after your parents died. All that was good in my heart, I guess, just dried up. I am embarrassed by my behavior and I hope that you could find it in your heart to forgive me.

My longtime friend David Birkshire will be contacting you, as he is the executor of my estate. Watuppa Grove is now under your loving care. Following your dreams is important Vanessa, and I know you will teach that to your children, so they too can find their voice and their sacred place in the world.
I love you Vanessa and your chickabiddies,
Grammy

✷✷✷✷✷✷

Vanessa's entire body shook with overwhelming emotion as her gaze reached for the river and her body filled with agonizing grief. Her memories continued to linger toward the river until she felt she conjured something hiding in her past. *Was Claire's story about, Claire, Grammy or me, or is it about all of us?* Staring down slope to the river, Vanessa continued to chew on her thoughts

Later that morning, as her and the children went to work on the last piece of the puzzle, the last secret compartment. After about ten minutes, Brodie remembered Grammy saying, that one compartment in the box could be opened by a sharp object in a pinhole. Suddenly he noticed a very small pinhole in the steel. Taking one of the needles from the sewing kit, Brodie inserted it, which then released a spring, and the contents of the final secret compartment were revealed. The room drank in the silence. The contents were fifteen handwritten pages, folded but not yet bound together. Alongside, they found three small Mayan charms carved from a striking blue jade. One by one the pieces met the light of the retreating morning, a butterfly, a hummingbird, and a dragonfly each glistening, ancient and proud.

Maeve picked up the pages and began to read what appeared to be the end of Claire's story.

63

In the universe, there are things that are known,
and things that are unknown, and in between, there are doors.

—Ray Manzarek

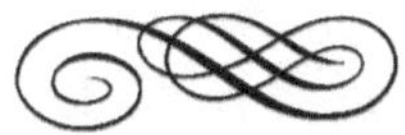

Philippe and I worked every day together, sharing the daily toil of running a successful business. By December, we found ourselves overwhelmed by it all, deprived of sleep and exhausted by the sheer drama of the bakery. Frustrated, worn, and still very sad, we argued about nothing. Daniel's sudden death had had a traumatic impact on both of us.

One night we realized a mistake in our supply order, and an argument boiled over.

"I can't keep doing this, Philippe, the baking, the constant working, and catering to so many unsavory characters. I am losing my mind, I must get away from here."

I began pounding my fists into Philippe's chest in frustration. Philippe grabbed both of my flailing arms and then kissed me. I, of course, was caught off guard at first, but after a short, quick breath, I folded into what I needed most.

From that moment we were linked, both by our future and our past. Philippe and I slid easily into a routine of romance and work. Over the winter we shared our stories and our belongings. We each chose something from each other's belongings, one at a time. I loved the pearls, especially after Philippe said Daniel had bought them for me before he knew I was married, even though Daniel had maintained that he purchased them for his mother. Philippe admired my pair of Derringer pistols and said, "Have these ever been fired?"

"I doubt it, Ashley was a businessman who never put himself at risk. Everything he did was calculated like a ledger."

Philippe tossed a piano key to me and said, "I picked this up the day they smashed your piano."

As I held the key in my hand, my mind meandered back to the smashing of my piano and the altercations that followed. I thought of all those piano lessons, which I'd resisted like a stubborn mule. I now realized that it had sent my life in a different direction. It all now seemed so very clear.

Philippe, his face sagging, said, "This is all I have of my father's, a piece of deer hide." He tossed it to me, and began to light his cigar.

After some examination, I said, "Philippe, this is a map. You are aware of this, right?"

"Of course I am aware of that, but a map to where?"

"Just a minute, I think I have what we need." I began to rummage through my belongings, and then slapped down a bundle of maps on the table in front of Philippe. "These, my friend, are Ashley's maps." As I laid them out, I said, "Which one looks like your father's map?"

Philippe pointed to one and I said, "Yucatán."

"What?"

"Yucatán, southern Mexico on the Caribbean side. There is a river here, see?"

"Yes?"

"It goes into the interior a ways. What is this drawing, pointing at it? It looks like an hourglass, covered with an upside-down U."

"Yes, but what is it? What does it mean?"

"Perhaps it's a cave," I said. "Maybe the hourglass is the shape of the cave entrance? Was your father a pirate?"

"So I have heard."

"He left this for you and your mother, and she gave it to you?"

"Yes, Claire, I told you that."

"Philippe, this is your father's map to his treasure!"

"Do you really think so?"

64

Each friend represents a world in us, a world not born until they arrive, and it is only by this meeting that a new world is born.

—Anais Nin

Every two weeks, Moon Bear would arrive at the bakery from Sacramento with bundles of herbs for the bakery. She usually traveled alone, but this time she had brought Chang with her.

Stepping onto the boardwalk, they met three miners walking out of the bakery. The men stopped and glared at Chang and Moon Bear, their eyes on the sack of herbs.

One man stepped forward and said, "Hey, coolie scum, it appears you and your squaw are lost. China is that way." He pointed to the west.

Moon Bear, with a defiant glaze, moved to Chang's flank, her eyes piercing and focused on the men. Chang stood his ground, his face calm.

From inside the bakery Philippe's jackboots hammered on planks of Douglas fir as he called out, "Chang, Moon Bear!" Giving his friends a hug, Philippe noticed the men, their stare lingering with disgust.

"Is there a problem here, gentlemen?" Turning to his friends, he said, "I hope they have been respectable toward you."

Chang bowed, first to Philippe and then to the men, and said, "They have been most gracious." He then walked into the Hang Town Bakery on nimble feet.

"Hello, Moon Bear, nice to see you again."

"Where is Claire?" Moon Bear asked.

"She is resting; she begins baking at midnight you know. She should be here soon for closing. You are staying for dinner, right? Please join us. So, what brings you to Hang Town, my friends?"

"I'm branching out my healing practice," Chang replied.

Moon Bear chided, "You are becoming an old lazy dog." Her eyes, the color of black walnut, shimmered like stars on a moonless night. "It's good for you to move through the world." Glancing back to Philippe, she said, "I told him he needed a good scamp or the fleas would consume his flesh."

"I am old, this is true. This is a path we all must travel and this young lady here remembers her dreams of the future, so if she says walk, I walk. Together we balance our chi."

"Let me take the herbs back and I will pour you both some tea." After retrieving the bundle of herbs from Moon Bear, Philippe turned and disappeared to the back of the bakery.

Moon Bear said, "Chang, come here, I want to show you these cakes and breads. The last time I was here, Claire gave me some to take back but I ate them all on the way home."

"I knew there was a reason to come to Hang Town. It's the only time I will get try taste any of them."

65

Sadness is but a wall between two gardens.

—Kahlil Gibran

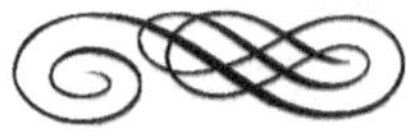

I entered through the back of the bakery and was greeted by the welcomed warmth of the ovens and Philippe pouring tea. I was pleased to hear that Moon Bear had returned with her herbs and pleasantly surprised that Chang had come with her. I had become fond of them both and felt as though Philippe and I would be lost without them. They had been our caregivers in the days after returning from Golden Sun Mountain pool. I went to the front and found them both in front of an almost-empty case of cakes.

"Moon Bear, Chang welcome, what a pleasant surprise. How did she convince you to join her, Chang?"

"Remember those cakes you gave her last time to bring to me— well, she ate them before she got home," Chang teased.

Moon Bear shot a sly smile me as I reached into the case for the last of the cakes and said, "Follow me, Philippe is pouring the tea."

After a meal of venison, beets, and potatoes, we sipped port with an apple crisp. Moon Bear refused to sip poison, but enjoyed my dessert.

"Philippe and I are going to take a trip," I told them.

"To where?" Chang asked.

"We are going to the Caribbean Sea."

"Why?" Chang asked.

"Philippe's father was a pirate." Philippe tensed and he placed his hand on my knee as to say, *stop this conversation,* which I did not. "His name was Jean Laffite. I believe he left Philippe the map to his treasure, and we will soon be off to find it."

Chang gazed at Philippe, handing him a cigar then lighting his own. After a long drag, he said, "I have heard of your father. Anyone who has traveled the seas knows of him. Some believe he was a hero and others a criminal."

"What do you think my father was, Chang? A hero, or a criminal?" Lighting his cigar, Philippe continued, "He certainly was not a father."

"I cannot say about your father, other than that he must have been a good man because he chose a good woman and you have developed into a fine young man."

"Either way," I said, "We need a break from the bakery and the cold of winter."

"Can we help you with the bakery while you are gone?" Chang asked.

"We have worked out a deal with the two women who work for us. We will still need your herbs, Moon Bear. We think both of you should enjoy our cakes."

Moon Bear, her eyes dancing in the candlelight, said, "You both will have a safe journey and will discover what it is you seek."

66

The purpose of life is to live it, to taste experience to the utmost,
to reach out eagerly and without fear
for a newer and richer experience.

—ELEANOR ROOSEVELT

One month later, Philippe and I left our two employees in charge of the bakery and took off on a jaunt following Philippe's father's map. We waited at the dock to board the *SS Oregon,* a sister ship of the *California.* It was a cold February morning and the late winter wind lapped whitecaps on the bay tide. As we waited for the tide to shift, I put my hands to my face and began to cry. Philippe embraced me close, shifting my hair from my face, his eyes searching for an answer.

"What is wrong, Claire?"

"It's Ashley, Philippe. I just realized this is where he died. He was a good, honest man. God rest his soul." I sank into him and quietly collected myself..

The *Oregon* fortunately had not been pillaged of her eloquence by a plundering group of wild savages, unlike the *California.* Her lines were sleek, with three masts, two decks, and a dragon's head. The staterooms and lounge were impressive, and the deck chairs were comfortable. We settled into the voyage, very much aware of how different the set of circumstances were from our last voyage. We kept to ourselves and to our stateroom, playing dominoes and chess and reading to each other. I often thought of my piano and how, unknown to me then, yet obvious to me now, it had offered a tranquil respite in my self-imposed depression.

It took the *Oregon* only seventeen days, over turbulent and contentious seas, before it entered Panama City, anchored mountains with a bountiful green curtain of jungle against a striking blue horizon. As before, hundreds of men perched on the docks like a flock of angry birds needing a fresh meal, waiting to get to the gold fields.

Stepping onto the dock, I reached for Philippe's hand and said, "How luxurious to be here already. After spending three months at sea, seventeen days seems like a float down a river on a summer day."

Although it was the middle of winter, the humidity camped on our shoulders with each step.

I began to fan myself and said, "I forgot about the heat."

"We'll get used to it. We have at least two more weeks of it." Philippe's eyes searched out something safe, and he spotted a short man, with a week-old growth of gray beard, his face round, yet chiseled with the years. "Excuse me, can you help us? My wife and I are looking for a place to eat some food."

"Of course, my friend, follow me, we are almost there. I am Don Pedro."

Holding out his hand, Philippe said, *"Esta es mi esposa, Claire, y yo soy Philippe, un placer conocerte."* I asked what he had said and he whispered, "This is my wife, Claire, and I am Philippe, nice to meet you."

"Why do you keep calling me your wife?"

"Claire," he said, smiling his chiseled smile, "it is just easier. I am certainly not going to masquerade as your brother."

"I am not ready to get married, to anyone, just so we are clear."

With a wink, Philippe said, "Aye, aye captain."

Don Pedro, his hat weathered and tattered, had a crippled gait and a smile that revealed broken and missing teeth. We followed him up a hill to a small lean-to house with a woman cooking on a wood fire in the shade. A pregnant sow laid in a small enclosure next to a corral of mules. Monkeys chattered from the trees above as we approached. Flying insects wrestled midflight in the drones of heat. The light of the day was slowly evaporating, as Don Pedro's wife, Hortensia, stirred a large pot of *sancocho,* her shadow stretched across the yard, her small, stout frame and thick braid of hair silhouetted there.

Philippe and I learned over the meal that Don Pedro, like many men in Panama City, was in the business of transporting people to the Chagres River and was leaving for there with his mules the next morning. Don Pedro called the route Camino Real, the Royal Road. Both names referenced the Spanish, the road on which they transported their stolen Inca gold.

The next morning, the jungle awoke with the heat at sunrise. We followed the Royal Road into the highlands of jungle, where families slashed and burned an area for more sunlight to grow papaya, banana, beans, and corn. Riding the mules brought a soothing rhythm that was comforting and familiar. For a good part of the morning, Philippe recounted his story, before meeting me on the *California.* He told me about New Orleans, Gracie Métoyer, and crossing the isthmus. Then I told Philippe all about my parents, uncle, Leland, Watuppa Pond, Bluebell, and Sweet Pea, all the while Don Pedro softly singing Spanish ballads.

Philippe and I, over time, whether conscious of it or not, had stopped talking about Daniel, as if we both were afraid to reopen the wound. Our lives, now merged by tragedy, moved forward, determined to not look back. I thought of Daniel every day, clinging to a shimmer of memory, and I always arrived at the same place. Daniel and Ashley were so similar that I had almost known in my heart the outcome. Eventually I arrived at the fact that, like Ashley, perhaps I never really loved Daniel. Perhaps this was just an attempt at survival, but as Philippe painted his story on the Royal Road to Cruces, I knew that Philippe was different from both Ashley and Daniel.

In late afternoon we rode into Cruces and stopped at the home of Deloras, Don Pedro's sister, to spend the night. The next morning, Don Pedro took us to the river, where his nephew, Juan Carlos, would transport us downriver to Chagres by bungo. Over another pot of *sancocho*, Don Pedro teased his nephew then commended him on his bravery.

"I would fall off a mule any day, yet to fall out of the bungo and be a *cocodrilo* meal, no thank you."

Dozing after the meal and ten miles on a mule, I was transported back into the conversation. "Excuse me, what did he just say?"

"He said *cocodrilo*, crocodile."

"Crocodile! I am not riding in a bungo, whatever that is, with crocodiles swimming in the river."

"We each have a job, Señora Claire," Juan Carlos told me. "I will steer the bungo, you will tap on the side of the boat with a rock, and Señor Philippe will be in front with his rifle. This is how it is done. No worries, Señora, it is not mating season."

"Why did you not ever mention this to me, Philippe?"

"Well, for one, I forgot about the crocodiles. Besides," he continued with a loving smile, "I believe that this little jaunt we are on was your idea."

"Yes, but I am still terrified."

"If I were you, I would worry about the monkeys."

"What about the monkeys?" My eyes were like two saucers.

"When I was here before the monkeys threw fruit at us, protecting their territory, I presume."

"But why?"

"A few of the men in our party shot their pistols at them, for target practice, I suppose."

That night, the heat pressed down on me as I lay under the canopy of a large mango tree. My mind wandered until I found sleep, where I floated down the river being attacked by crocodiles and monkeys.

Outside of Cruces there was a stretch of rapids, and the dry season made its passage dangerously difficult. Juan Carlos assured us both that it was safe. After we watched several other bungos navigate the rapids safely, one bungo hit a boulder and lost a bit of cargo. As I watched a small box floating downriver, a chill of uneasiness spread across my skin.

Despite my objections, we were off on the next leg of our journey. The rapids were frightening to me and several times the bungo glanced lightly off the boulders, yet I found that Juan Carlos was right, it was safe.

Once floating on the River Chagres, I was in awe of the incredible beauty of the jungle, its colorful birds, and monkeys jumping from tree to tree, following the bungo. The newness of it all sucked me farther into the adventure. The river's calm began to ebb away my stress, and as we floated I pondered my fate. The events of the last year had changed me in a way I had yet to fully understand. I was a stronger woman, more resilient. I began to feel a confidence about my place in the world.

Three days later, we arrived in Chagres and the azure blue Caribbean. We slept on the beach in a grove of palm trees, and the next day Juan Carlos left to find Don Jose Menchaca, the oldest elder in Las Cruces, who had met a man once who fished the sea and dived for pearls near the town of Rio Balis.

For the first time during our short time together, Philippe and I finally began to really relax. We lounged leisurely on the beach, eating fish and fruits we had never imagined. After two days, Juan

Carlos arrived at the beach in a *jangada,* with Don Jose Menchaca and enough supplies for two weeks.

All I could say was, "My God, Philippe, you have got to be kidding. How far are we sailing in this raft?"

But we soon learned that we would travel in the *jangada* to a steamer moored beyond the reef. Relieved, I leaned in and kissed Philippe on the cheek.

The *jangada* provided ample transport to the paddle steamer, the *Conway,* but I teasingly asked, "Where should I sit, on the bananas?"

Smiling his wild grin, Philippe said, "Yes, I think the green ones will be better."

"Yes, the green bananas, they do look the most comfortable." As I settled onto the green bananas, alacrity filled my uneasiness when a small butterfly of cobalt rested next to me, its wings swaying. A moment later, as it flew away, I thought, *I will be safe.* The butterfly's visit left me empowered and I settled in for the next leg of the adventure.

As we set off on the *jangada,* I found myself searching my life and the events that had brought me to this moment. I was no longer Claire from Boston. That girl had vanished with Ashley's death. I was no longer the young woman I was with Daniel. For the first time in my young life I was learning to grasp control. Or as Levi would say, I appeared to be getting my ducks in a row.

The *Conway* had been built in England as a transport ship to the Caribbean islands—pretty much everything from mail to rum, tea to spices. It was a well-worn workhorse, listing on the side of tired.

On our first day moving north, I said, the *Conway* may not have the elegance of the *Oregon,* but still, the absence of crocodiles on the water is refreshing."

"Yes, that is true, Claire, but now we have sharks."

Three days later we arrived in Belize, where a deep, undulating jungle rose from the sea, dripping with anticipation of the unknown.

67

Sometimes the questions are complicated and the answers are simple.

—Dr. Seuss

On the way back home in the car, as fruit trees blurred outside the window, Maeve and Brodie bantered back and forth as to whether Claire and Philippe had found the pirate treasure.

Then Brodie asked, "Mom, what does it feel like to die? Does it hurt?"

"People all die differently, and under many different circumstances. Grammy passed in her sleep and that must have been very peaceful."

Brodie said, "When I die, I want to die like Grammy, peaceful."

Maeve playfully shouted, "Aye, aye, mate," and she used her arm as a sword, "you shall die by my pirate sword. Arrgh!"

"That is not funny, Maeve!" Brodie said, but Vanessa could hear the smile in his voice.

Driving down the road, listening to Maeve reading *A Wrinkle in Time* to her brother, Vanessa drifted back to the previous day, her Grammy beaming like a seven-year-old with a popsicle on a hot August day. She thought of Claire and her story, and of her own story, and wondered whether past lives could collide together and perhaps actually recycle themselves.

Staring back at her two children in the rearview mirror, her body filled toward the future, her heart full with the moment. She remembered her Grammy saying, "Have I told you how much I love you today?"

Looking out at the road ahead of her, she said, "Yes, you have, Grammy, and we love you, too."

About the Author—

Gary Griffith became captivated with California History while in the fourth grade and interpreting history became a life passion. He has been fortunate to teach California and U.S. History for many years to hundreds of emerging young writers since 1988. Gary lives in the Sonoma Valley, with his wife Patty.

www.ingramcontent.com/pod-product-compliance
Lightning Source LLC
Chambersburg PA
CBHW031236120726
47905CB00002B/623